Long Ago

AND

Far Away

ANGELO THOMAS CRAPANZANO

Inquiries and Book Orders should be addressed to:

Great Writers Media
Email: info@greatwritersmedia.com
Phone: (302) 918-5570

ISBN: 978-1-957148-95-3 (sc)
ISBN: 978-1-957148-96-0 (ebk)

Rev 3/10/2022

CONTENTS

DEDICATION

I wish to dedicate this book to all the Philippine people
who took care of me when I was stationed there,
and to Mia who was instrumental in talking
me into writing this novel.

CHAPTER ONE

His First Love

Gino sat at his desk deep in thought. He had his desk across from his bed. He lived upstairs from his parents with his aunt Stella and Uncle Joe. Aunt Stella could not have children, so she had an extra bed room in her two bed room apartment. When Gino's sister got too big to share a bed room with Gino, Gino moved upstairs with his Aunt and Uncle Joe. This evening he was trying to do his homework, but he could not concentrate on it. His thought kept going to the fact that he had no girlfriend. He didn't even have a girl that he could date. Now he was in his senior year and had no one to take to the graduation ball. His friend Nick had fixed him up with a date a couple of times but that didn't work out. He didn't want to take his sister so he had to find someone. Finally he decided to forget it for now and continue doing his homework. It was about eleven when his Aunt Stella came into his bed room.

"I am about to go to bed," said Aunt Stella. "I thought you would like an apple before you go to bed."

"Thank you," said Gino as he took a break from his homework. He loved Aunt Stella. She always brought him something before she went to bed. She was like a second mother to him. After she left her kindness gave him what he needed to go back to doing his homework. Completing his homework he went to bed.

The next day was Friday. After class, as Gino got home he got a phone call from his friend Nick.

"How are you doing?" asked Nick. "Do you have any plans for this evening?"

"No." answered Gino. "When have I ever had plans for Friday night?"

"You never know," answered Nick.

"Don't you have a date with Pat as usual?" asked Gino being surprised by Nicks comment.

"She has gone to Jeannette Pennsylvania," said Nick. "She has a cousin who is getting married tomorrow. I thought this would be a chance we boys could get together. I talked to Jim and his girlfriend has other plans also. He would be glad to come with us. We can go to our favorite restaurant and then go to a movie. The Imperial Theater has a great science fiction movie, called, '*A Time Before The End.*' It is about a time before the great flood. Let's get together and have dinner and afterwards go to the movie. After the movie we can go to 'Night Owl' and have a hamburger and a drink"

"Sound great to me," answered Gino. "When do we get together?"

"I'll pick up Jim at five and get you at about five fifteen. Is that ok with you?"

"Sounds great," said Gino. "I'll be ready. I get home about four thirty so I will have plenty of time to get ready."

As Nick promised, he was at Gino's house at five fifteen. After the normal salutations the three went to a local restaurant and then went to the theater. The theater was almost empty. There were about ten people up front and about six people in the middle. They decided to sit in the back. They liked that so that they would not disturb any one and no one would disturb them. They had only sat in their seat for a few minutes when they hear giggling and soft laughter behind them. Nick turned around looked at them. Nick was a gentle up beat person. He wasn't angry with them.

"Hi girls," Nick commented. "What is so funny? Why don't you let us in on the joke?"

"Jill here said that her math teacher must have come from the same period as the guy in this movie," said the girl in the middle as they all laughed. "My name is Betty and the girl on my left is Jill and the girl on the end is Carol. Who are you guys?"

"My name is Nick and the guy on my left is Jim. The other guy is Gino." After some small talk the movie started. After the movie as the girls got up to leave Nick addressed them.

"Look girls," Nick started. "We are going to 'Night Owl' for a hamburger and a drink. We are not asking for any long term relationships. We are three guys out on a boy's night out. It would be nice to have three beautiful girls to enjoy the evening with."

"We planned on going to McDonalds for a hamburger and a coke. We like McDonald's hamburgers," said Betty who it seemed was the leader of the group.

"What do you think fellows?" said Nick turning to his fellow companions.

"McDonalds sounds good to me," said Jim.

"It's ok with me," answered Gino.

"Unless you fellows want a beer or stronger drink," asked Jill.

"No," said Nick. "We are not beer or liquor drinkers. We were only going to have a soft drink also."

"I don't know," said Jill. "We don't know you fellas. You may be trouble."

"How can we be trouble," asked Jim. "You will be going in your car and we will be going in our car. We will not be in the same place until we get to the same restaurant. This could happen any time with lots of people. We are just going to share the same table."

"We can just pretend we don't know you until we get to the restaurant," said Nick. "We will meet there and just share the same table"

"This could happen to anyone except with us there is one advantage," said Gino. "And that is that we will pay the bill." They all laughed. They thought that the whole conversation was funny.

"Look," said Jill. "Let's not be silly. Let's all go to the McDonalds as new friends." With that they left, got into their cars and proceeded to McDonalds. When they got there they found that there were only two tables available. One was for four people and the other was for two. Fortunately they were together.

"Carol and I will sit in the smaller table," said Gino. "I think we would like to get to know each other better. Neither one of us have had a chance to joined in the conversation." Nick sat next to Jill and

Jim sat next to Betty. They each ordered their hamburgers to their own liking. All three couples had their own individual conversations. Gino and Carol could hear the others talking and laughing. They were all having a good time. Gino liked Carol and he could tell that she was attracted to him. Every time he would look at her she would look down at her dish. Carol was slim and very beautiful. Gino loved her eyes. They were a shade between brown and blue, just a little lighter than hazel. Her hair was a lovely light brown.

"Carol," started Gino. "My name is Gino Cozano. I would like to know more about you. What are your plans for the future? That will tell me a lot about you."

"I haven't thought too much about it," said Carol. "My name is Caroline Calmer. I do like to help people. I may consider going to nursing school after I graduate from high school. I just started high school, you know."

"What do you like to do when you are free from school work? What is your hobby?"

"I like to go to movies and I love to dance," said Carol. "I don't have a hobby, but enough about me. What are your plans for the future? What do you want to be when you graduate?"

"So much depends on the war," said Gino. "I'm sure that as soon as I graduate I will be drafted into the army. When I get out I would like to go to college and study to b an engineer."

"That sounds fantastic," said Carol. "What kind of engineer do you want to be and why?"

"I think I want to be an Electronic Engineer," explained Gino. "I was fascinated with the thought of a video pictures being sent through the air. That is an amazing technology."

"Sounds like a fantastic dream," said Carol. "Do you have what it takes to achieve this?"

"I hope so," answered Gino. "I have always had high grades in both math and science."

"Both intelligent and handsome," said Carol smiling.

"So you think I'm handsome?" asked Gino. Carol only smiled. "Well I think you are beautiful so if you are attracted to me and I'm attracted to you, then we must get together again soon."

"What are you saying?" asked Carol.

"I'm asking you for your phone number," said Gino, "so that I could call you and ask you for a date."

"I'm right here," said Carol, "so why don't you ask me now? By the way I don't go out on school nights."

"So what are you doing this Friday?" asked Gino.

"I'm free," answered Carol. "What do you have in mind?"

"I would like to take you to dinner and then to a nice movie," said Gino.

"I would like that," answered Carol. "What time do you want to pick me up?"

"First you had better give me your address and phone number," said Gino. Carol opened her purse and pulled out a piece of paper and a pen. She wrote down what Gino had asked for and handed it to him.

"Now can you tell me what time you will pick me up?" said Carol with laughter in her vice.

"Your funny," said Gino, "how about five this Friday?"

"I can hardly wait," said Carol. At that they both laughed. After some small talk they realized that it had b come very late. Finally they all said goodbye and left. Gino was very happy. He now had someone to date and to take to Nicks parties.

It seemed to Gino that Friday would never come. Finally it was Friday. He got home from school, took a shower and shaved. He wanted to look his best on their first date. He walked up to the front door and rang the doorbell. A lovely older woman opened the door.

"How can I help you?" she said.

"My name is Gino. I have a date with Carol."

"Come on in," said the woman. "I'm Carol's mother."

"Thank you Mrs. Calmer" said Gino as he walked in.

"Your name is Gino?" asked the woman. "Isn't that Italian?"

"Yes it is," said Gino. "My grandparents are from Sicily."

"All Italians are Catholic aren't they?" asked Mrs. Calmer.

"Yes they are," answered Gino. "But all in my family are Baptist. We are Born Again Christians."

"That is good to know," said Mrs. Calmer, "We go to a Baptist church also. While we wait for her I would like to know more about you. What are your plans for the future?"

"I would like to be an Electronic Engineer, but who knows," said Gino. "I'm sure that as soon as I graduate I will be drafted into the war."

"Please stop interrogation my date," said Carol walking into the room.

We are just having a conversation," said Carols mother in her defense.

"Sorry I'm late," said Carol. "I need to be in by midnight." She looked a smiled at her mother notifying her ahead of time.

"Let's go then," said Gino, "nice to have met you, Mrs. Calmer." With that they left.

"I hope my mother's curiosity didn't bother you," said Carol.

"No," said Gino. "She is just trying to protect you. It tells me that you are a loving family. Where would you like to go for dinner?"

I feel like some fish, perhaps some shrimp," said Carol. "I haven't had fish for a while."

"There is a Red Lobster, not too far from here," said Gino. "If you want we can go there."

"Sounds great to me," answered Carol. After that Gino drove to the Red Lobster Restaurant. They had a special that week. It was a dinner with three different types of shrimps. Both Carol and Gino ordered that dish. Gino also ordered a bowl of their special clam chowder soup. He asked for an empty cup and he shared the soup with Carol.

That was great," said Gino. They both enjoyed the dinner very much. After dinner they headed for the center of town where all the theaters were. As they drove by Carol pointed to the Cleveland Civic Theater.

"That looks like an interesting movie," she said. "It is called *The Fox and The Lamb*. Let's go see it." Gino parked the car and they went in to see the movie. After the movie they started to go back towards the east side of town.

"Do you want stop and have a hamburger and a soda," asked Gino.

"I would love to but it is getting too late," said Carol. "Remember I have to be in by midnight. We don't have time to eat and make it home by twelve."

"I will agree if you promise that I will get another chance to take you there," said Gino

"Just take me home," said Carol with a big smile on her face. When they got to her house, Gino walked her to the front door.

"I enjoyed this evening very much," said Gino. "I will like to do this again."

"I would like that very much," said Carol. "I don't go out during the week. I date on Fridays and Saturdays. I prefer Fridays. Saturdays I like to go to bed early because I have to get up early to go to church."

"I will pick you up Friday at about five," said Gino. "Therefore, until then, good night,"

"Aren't you going to kiss me good night?" asked Carol.

"I thought it was improper to do it on the first date," answered Gino.

"This is our second date," said Carol. "Didn't we triple date last Friday? Besides, there is no one looking. I won't tell if you won't." Gino didn't have to be asked twice. He put his hand on her shoulders and pulled her into his arms. Then he slowly moved in until his lips touched hers. Gino was surprised at how passionately she reacted to the kiss. She wrapped her arms around him and squeezed tightly. Gino enjoyed the kiss very much and was thrilled to have her in his arms, but he didn't get the butterflies he expected from the stories he had heard. Then he told himself that it is only a story told in the movies. People don't get butterflies. He didn't see how he could be more excited. After a few seconds that s emed like minutes they parted and she went inside. Gino left feeling great. He now had a date that he could take to some of Nick's parties.

Gino called her on Wednesday to say hello and to confirm his date that coming Friday. She seemed to like that he called. After a short conversation Gino hung up. Friday came and Gino was at Carol's house exactly at five. Carol answered the door and was ready to go. They had a delicious dinner and then were ready to go to a movie.

"Gino can I make a suggestion?" asked Carol.

"Of course," said Gino. "I take it you don't want to go see a movie. I was thinking the same thing. I checked the papers and didn't see a movie that I liked."

"It's not only that," said Carol. "I know of a nice place not too far from here that has nice music. I would like to go dancing."

"Where is this place and what is it called?"

"It is in Geneva," said Carol. "Actually it is nearer to Geneva on the Lake. It is a place called Cristal Ballroom. It has slow music and serves only soft drinks."

"That is pretty far away," said Gino.

"From your house but not as far from here," said Carol sweetly trying to convince Gino. "I just feel like dancing." Gino couldn't argue with that so he gave in.

"I think we have to leave early," said Gino. "Don't forget that I live about a half hour south of you." It took them over a half hour to get there. Gino was glad they went there. He enjoyed having his arms around her. Besides that, Gino loved to dance. They both had a Coke and danced until they were both tired. It was about ten when Carol suggested they leave.

"I think we have had more than enough dancing for now," said Carol. "I would like to spend a little time alone with you." Gino didn't really want to leave. It was too early he though. However he was not going to argue with her. They left and arrived at Carol's house about ten forty-five. We have about an hour to spend together," said Carol as she moved closer to Gino and wrapped her arms around him. Gino knew what she had in mind. He then put his arms around her and pulled her tight against him. With his right hand behind her head he pulled her in for a passionate kiss. When their lips touched Carol went wild. Gino was surprised at her action. Suddenly he felt her tongue forcing itself between his lips. Gino open his mouth and let her tongue in. Their tongues played together with wild movements. This went on for over an hour. Gino was surprised at her passionate behavior. She began rubbing her body against his with excitement. Gino realized that he had to end this before they both would do something they would regret. He then pushed her away and put her heard on his shoulder.

"We have to slow down and cool off," said Gino.

"Why?" asked Carol. "I trust you"

"I don't trust me," said Gino trying to let her off the hook. "Besides I want to save some of this for the next time."

"Ok," said Carol reluctantly. "I'm glad to hear that there will be a next time." She slowly pulled herself up sitting upright on the car seat. "Will you walk me to the door?" she asked.

"Of course," said Gino. "I'm looking forward to the good night kiss. The good night kiss was a normal lover's kiss. There was no passion. Gino laughed inside. The goodnight kiss will never be the same.

The next day was Saturday. Gino had no place to go so he slept in till eleven. After breakfast he decided to do his homework. He was going to have a test on Monday so he decided to study Sunday after church. Monday morning he got up early and studied the notes he took that he felt would be on the test. The class that gave the test was his second class, so he spent as much time as he could in his first class, when the teacher wasn't looking, studying his notes. He was dead set on passing this test. After the test, which he felt he passed he spent the rest of the day thinking of how passionate Carol was in the car Friday evening. On Wednesday he was about ready to call Carol when the phone rang. It was Nick.

"Hi old buddy," said Nick. "How are you?"

"First of all, I'm not old," said Gino kiddingly. "Other than that I am your buddy and I'm fine."

"Very funny," said Nick. "The reason I called is to invite you to a house party I am having at my house this Friday. If you can't get a date we can set you up with a friend of Pat's."

"Never again with your blind dates," said Gino. "Besides I have a date."

"Is that right" said Nick sounding skeptical. Gino did not date often and except when Pat got him a blind date Gino would never go to one of nick's parties. "Who are you dating?" He asked.

"I'm dating a girl named Carol. You met her at the theater and later at McDonald. I've dated her twice already and I have a date with her this Friday. In fact I was about to call her when you called. I want to confirm our date."

"That great," said Nick. "I'm so glad to hear that. We will see you Friday then?"

"I will do my best," said Gino. "She likes to go dancing."

"That's fine," said Nick. "Tell her that after a small dinner will spend the rest of the evening dancing."

"We are having a dinner too," said Gino. "What are we having?"

"I'm not sure yet, but I think Pat has cheeseburgers in mind," said Nick.

That Friday Gino picket up Carol at five as planned

"Where are we going to eat this evening?" asked Carol.

"We are going to a special place to have a short dinner and then we are going to dance all night," said Gino. "It's a surprise night."

"Come on now, where are we going?" asked Carol. When he didn't answer she continued. "Have we been there before?"

"Nope," said Gino. "But I hope if you like it we will go again the next time it's available."

"You mean that it is not always open?" asked Carol.

"It's open all the time but there will not always be dancing," answered Gino.

"They only have dancing on Friday," asked Carol?

"Well here we are," said Gino as he pulled into Nick driveway. "You will soon find out everything." They were met at the front door by Nick and Pat. They went inside and Carol was introduced to Nick and Pat. As they entered the living room they were introduced to everyone there. Gino knew most of the couples there. The music was playing and some couples were dancing. Nick then went to the tape player and shut off the music.

"Now that everyone is here, we should take time and eat dinner" said Nick. "We have regular hamburgers and some cheeseburgers. Please get in line, get a plate, and pick whatever you like." Gino picked a cheeseburger but Carol picked a regular burger. They filled their plate with all the different vegetables and a soft drink and sat down to eat. After they ate Nick turn on the soft slow music they love. Everyone started to dance. Everyone but Jim and his girlfriend Betty loved the music. Jim and Betty wanted some fast music. Nick appeased them every once in a while but slow music was the preferred music by everyone. At about ten Carol asked to go home. Gino hesitated because he knew what she wanted to do. He enjoyed the sessions but he had never done this before with any girl. It was new to him and he was afraid that it would go too far. Gino hesitated as long as he could but finally they left. When he parked in Carol's house drive he pulled in so that he was near the front door. He hoped that her mother would see them and call her in. Carol went directly into her act.

"I wanted to leave early because I wanted to spent time in your arms," said Carol. Gino didn't have time to respond because her lips pressed hard against his. They stayed there for more than an hour. Gino felt uncomfortable when his passion got higher than he had ever experienced before. Suddenly Gino pulled her away from him.

"Honey," he said. "You had better go in. Your mother said that I should have you home by eleven. It is now past eleven thirty. Your mother is going to get angry and not let me date you again. I don't want that to happen, so please go in. I will walk you to the door so that I could give you a goodnight kiss."

"I guess you are right," said Carol. Gino walked her to the door but he didn't get a chance to kiss her goodnight. Carol's mother opened the door as they got there.

"You are late," said Carol's mother. Before she could answer Gino broke in.

"I so sorry," he answered her. "We were at a house party and lost count of time. It will never happen again." Carol's mother didn't answer. She just grabbed Carol by the arm and brought her inside. Gino was happy that it happened. Now he had good reason to shorten their romantic auto sessions. Although he felt relieved he was worried that he would miss the long sessions in the car.

The next two week went by as usual. Gino got Carol home by eleven and managed to keep their car passion to less than an hour. It was on the next week that Gino got a call from Nick.

"Hi Gino," said Nick. "How would you like to go on a picnic?"

"Are you kidding," answered Gino. "It is fall and the temperature will be in the upper thirties. We will freeze to death."

"It will be inside the State park cabin," answered Nick. "It has a large fireplace where we can cook hot dogs and I will bring my disk player and we can dance the rest of the night."

"When do you want to go?" asked Gino.

"Well we have to get out by eleven o'clock," said Nick, "so we had better get there by five if we want to do some dancing."

"What day do you want to go," asked Gino?

"How about Friday the twelfth," said Nick. "That's about a week away."

"Sounds great," said Gino. "I will call Carol to make sure she will be available. I'll keep in touch." After Gino hung up, he called Carol.

"Hi Carol. How are you?"

"I'm fine," Carol answered. "What do you have in mind?"

"How would you like to go to a picnic," said Gino. "We have never gone to a picnic together."

"Are you kidding?" said Carol. "It is going to be too cold to be outside. You go. I'll pass." Gino then explained that it was going to be inside a park cabin and that they would have a fireplace where they could cook hot dogs.

"I think it will be fun," said Gino.

"I'm not sure I will like it," said Carol. "I would rather be alone with you. When is it?"

"It will be on the twelfth," said Gino. "We can be alone this Friday. We can make up for the following Friday." That Friday Gino and Carol did make up the time in the car for two Fridays.

On the next Friday Gino picked up Carol and they went to the State Park cabin for the picnic. When they got there Nick with his date and Ray with his date were the only ones there. They introduced themselves to everyone and Gino turned to Nick.

"We are a little early," said Gino to Nick.

"What is important is that you are here," said Nick. "Why don't you joined Pat and me and set your stuff here on the floor by our blanket and you guys could help me start the fire."

"I think Sara and I will set our blanket at the other side of the fire place," said Ray. "It is out of the way. When we get settled I'll come and help you with the fireplace fire."

Ray did as he said. He then joined Gino in cooking his hot dogs over the now hot fire. They were the only two that cooked in the fire place. All the others brought sandwiches. They all enjoyed there dinner on the floor each on their own blanket. After they ate Nick turned on his record player and they all danced. The evening went faster than they wanted. It was a quarter to eleven when Nick turned off the music.

"I think we better start getting all our things together," said Nick. "We have to be out of here by eleven." Everyone did as Nick suggested. After saying goodbye to each other, they all left. It was funny that as they all left they saw the State patrol office diving up to make sure they every one left by the required time. On the drive to Carol's house, Gino turned to Carol.

"Now, that wasn't that bad, was it?" he asked her.

"No," she answered, "I had a lot of fun. I love dancing with your arms around me. However, we will not have much time together in the car."

"You did tell your mother that we would not be home before twelve didn't you," asked Gino?

"Yes I did when you called and told me," said Carol. "It was OK with her."

"Well then," said Gino," we will have about a half hour to satisfy your yeaning's"

"I hope it is also your desire," said Carol with a smirking smile.

"Of course," said Gino. He decided he had better just change the subject. He did not enjoy it as much as she did. He was not used to that much passion. They got home about twenty minutes to twelve. They did not stop smooching until they saw Carol's mom by the front door.

Gino and Carol dated every Friday, some times in the early fall with Nick and Pat and Jim and Betty. Carol was OK with that knowing that soon Nick and Jim would be leaving for the service. Both

Nick and Jim were older than Gino and they were scheduled to get drafted in early January right after they graduated from high school. At Christmas time Carol had out of town relative stay with them. So Gino did not see her on Christmas weekend. He did give her a gift the Friday before Christmas and wished her a Merry Christmas. The same thing happened at New Years. In early January Gino went to Nick and Jim's graduation party. A couple of weeks later Nick was drafted into the army. Jim didn't want to be drafted. He enlisted in the navy. Carol had Gino all to herself after that. The weeks went by faster than Gino would have liked. It soon was Thanksgiving. Carol had a dinner with a large family gathering. So Gino didn't see her until the next Friday. It was the same thing for Christmas. Carol had relative visiting from out of town. Gino saw Carol the Friday before Christmas. He gave her a Christmas gift and didn't see her again until the Friday after the New Year. Soon it was May and Gino's graduation. Gino's family and his close relatives all went to the graduation proceedings. Gino next took Carol to the graduation dance. They had a great time. That evening when Gino took Carol home he got an unexpected surprise. After kissing her good night, Carol turned to Gino.

"Gino," she started, "Let's get married before you have to go into the service."

"Carol, are you serious?" said Gino. "First you are only sixteen. Next, your parents will not allow it. Besides, we will never have time to arrange a wedding. I already got a letter telling me to report to the Military recruiting office in down town Cleveland.

"We can sneak out and go down town and g t married by a judge," suggested Carol.

"Now you are being silly," said Gino. "The judge would want your parent's approval. Just forget it for now. What is your hurry? Let's give it some thought." On the way home Gino was disturbed by the thought of getting married. He had a lot of plans in what he wanted to do. He thought that with some military time he could get enough educational aid through the GI bill to get a college degree. When he got home he forgot about Carol. He wasn't sure he would want to marry her anyway.

To soon the day came when Gino had to repost to the military recruiting office. When he got there he found a line of men his age waiting there in the waiting room. After about an hour his name was called and asked to go into the main office. There he was examined by several Doctors. They were lined up so that as one fellow passed he would move over to the next doctor. One by one they went from one doctor to another. The first Doctor was a general physician. The next was a Dentist. After the dentist was an optometrist. Anyone that failed one of the tests was directed to a side office. As Gino was in line to see the general Physician, a young boy came out of the dentist office.

"I hope none of you guys have teeth problems," he said holding a bloody hanky to his mouth. "They don't fill a cavity they just pull the tooth." Gino was not worried. He had just had his teeth cleaned about a month ago. He thought however that it was a terrible thing to do. From the commotion he heard however, he was sure that other fellows were worried. After the medical examination they were sent to a new line. Gino understood that this was the line that they would be assign whether they would be Army soldiers, Navy men of Air Force members. Just as they got to the assigning officer Gino noticed that the fellow in front of him was assigned to the Navy. He had hopes that they would assign a few after him. However when he got up to the officer he was assign to the army. As he stood there wondering where to go next, he heard that the fellow behind him was assigned to the Air Force. That was just like his luck Gino thought. He went into a large room where several other men were waiting for further instruction. A few minutes later an Army Sargent came in and called the name of several men. They were asked to follow him. After they left another Sargent came in and called out names. Gino's name was one of them. The group with Gino was all led to a large room with desks. There they were told to take a seat and each got a test paper. They were told that they would take four different tests. They were given about a half hour for each test. After the tests they were give a sheet with directions to their next stop. An officer at the place they were directed told them the tests were over and given each a release sheet. The sheet stated that they had passed all the tests and were instructed to be in Detroit on Monday May 8th. It also gave them the day and hour that they were to assemble at the train station in Cleveland. It also said that they were not to bring a suitcase. Bring only one set of civilian clothes and underwear in a plastic bag.

The week went by too quickly. It was a very sad occasion saying goodbye to his mom and dad. His mother cried so bad that she almost passed out. Gino's dad and sister had to help her.

Later that day Gino found himself at the Detroit Army Base. He was assigned to a bunk in one of the cabins and told to relax and to report to the fitting room the next morning. At the fitting room Gino was fitted with an Army uniform and two pairs of Fatigues. He was also given a Duffle bag for his cloths. Gino was then told that he would be assigned a training camp in a few days. He was told to report to the front of the barracks every morning at 8 am. There they would then be given additional information. Usually about a dozen men were called, loaded on a truck and taken out of the area. Gino realized that this would soon be happening to him. The rest were dismissed and told that they were free for the rest of the day until 8 the next day, and not go too far from the area. This is where Gino met Vincent.

"Hi" said Gino as they both were leaving to return to their rooms. You are from Cleveland aren't you? I think I saw you on the train here.

"Yes" said Vincent. "I'm from Garfield Heights."

"I'm from Fairlawn. It is a suburb of Akron. Do you have any idea of what is going on?"

"I understand that we will be assigned to an Army training base. I think that not all of us would be assigned to the same base," said Vincent. "For now I guess we are free to do whatever we want until we are assigned," said Gino. Just outside the camp were several restaurants and a local bar.

"What do you say we will go to the bar and have a drink? I would love a glass of Dago Red."

"I'm sorry Gino," said Vincent. "I don't drink. Let's go to a movie"

"I don't drink more than a small glass of Wine around dinner. Mostly with my meal," said Gino in his defense. "I think we should have dinner first. A movie is at least two hours."

"I wonder," said Vincent as a sudden thought, "how far we are allowed get from the camp?"

"I understand that after we are dismissed in the morning, we will be free to go anywhere," said Gino. They did what Gino recommended. They ate at a nice restaurant and saw a detective movie.

It was three days later that after reporting to the front of the cabins that Gino and about a dozen other men were called and told to follow Corporal Windon. They were then loaded on a truck and taken directly to the train station. That was the last time that Gino saw Vincent. They were all led up one of the cars and seated.

"Corporal Windon," asked one of the men, "where are we going?"

"You are going to South Carolina," said Corporal Windon. "I will not be going with you. Someone will pick you up at the train stop and truck you down to Boot camp just east of Sumter." When the train conductor yelled "All Aboard" Corporal Windon got off and waved good bye.

It was late that evening that the train came to a stop. Gino had no idea where they were. All the soldiers and Gino were asked by a Sargent who came aboard to follow him. Gino was amazed to see about a hundred Solders that were leaving the area. Gino figured that they were done with their training and were going overseas. When they got to a military truck that was parked near the train station, they were asked to get in. After they drove for about an hour, they came to the army camp. They were all assigned a bed in one of the barracks. Ten men were assigned to each barracks. Gino was assigned to the first barrack. They were all told to come out at eight o'clock in the morning at the sound of the bugle. They were to wear fatigues.

The next morning at the sound of the bugle they were all lined up in front of the bunker. Gino was surprised at the number that lined up in front of the barracks. There were about 4 barracks on the area he was in. He figured that there were about forty men in the lineup. Suddenly a well-dressed officer stepped up to the mike.

"Attention," he yelled. "I am Captain Bogan. I am in charge of Company D. You are in Platoon 4. I am here today to welcome you to Camp Sumter training center. You will be here for four months. You will get four weekends off. This platoon will be under the control of Lieutenant Stillman." At that he turned the mike over to the lieutenant.

I am Lieutenant Stillman. I will be in charge of this area. At the end of the barracks you will see the Food Court. There are four squads under me. Each squad is under the control of a Sergeant. Because of the limited space and equipment of each training facility each squad will train separately. Each squad therefore will have a different schedule of training events. I will not be involved in your training so you will be under the direct control of your squad Sergeant."

Without any further delays let me turn you over to your Staff Sergeants." Standing behind the Lieutenant were four Sergeants who stepped forward. One who was the left move all the way left of the groups. He spoke first.

"My name is Sergeant Halisek. I am the leader of squad 101. Will the following persons please line up in front of me?" He then called out several names. Gino's name was one of the names he called out.

"Now all of you get in line and follow me," instructed the sergeant. He then march them into a field away from the other groups.

"The first thing we are going to do is to learn all the instruction and commands that you will be given." He started with what we were to do when he called us to attention. It took five minutes for him to describe all that we had to do and that there was a punishment if we didn't follow his call to attention. It took an hour for him to describe all the other commands that he could call out. We spent another hour practicing them. After he was satisfied he told us that we were at the place for our first Basic training area. It was the exercise area.

"What if we don't follow your instruction?" asked one of the members of the squad.

"You will still go overseas but you will be peeling potatoes the rest of your army career." said the sergeant. He then continued. "This is the first training location. There are nine more trainings events that you all have to go through. I will guide you through them all." After a few exercises he let them to the small cabin on the site. There he told them to pick up the eight pound weights. They did several exercises till noon. "Let all go to lunch," said the s rgeant. "We will do this every morning. Let's meet here at one after lunch fully armed."

After lunch they all hung around getting to know their fellow squad members. Gino got to be friendly with Andy Midiago. He was from Pittsburg Pennsylvania. At one they all met at the field as instructed.

"We are now going on a field trip," said the sergeant. "Line up in attention. Turn right March." They followed him, marching in tune with his number calling. It seemed like they marched about two or three miles until they got to the woods. "Advance Forward," yelled sergeant Halisek. Fortunately they had their bayonet with them. They cut their way through the thick brush until they got to the river. There was a wire stretched across the river. Above was another wire about five feet higher. "Cross over one at a time," yelled the sergeant.

"What are they trying to train us here?" questioned Andy to Gino. I don't think the enemy will have a wire across their rivers."

"Perhaps they are checking our ability to handle any occasion," said Gino. That evening they went to diner almost too tired to eat.

The next days were just as demanding. One day they were led through woods that ended at a twenty feet or more brick wall. There was a rope that was attached to the top and hung down to the ground. They were asked to climb up the wall using the rope and climb down the other side using a rope that was hanging down on the other side. They went through this several times during the next few weeks. The most frightening and dangerous training event however was the belly crawling under a netting that was barely a foot above ground and about twenty feet long, A machine gun was firing just above the netting. They were warned that the bullets flew just above the netting and they should not lift their head above the netting for it would cause a quick death. They had to do this several times. No one was hurt. Everyone kept his whole body tightly on the ground. Gino always kept his nose plowing through the dirt. It was about a month later that all four squads were called together. They were told to bring the full gear. Lt. Stillman took over. They all lined up facing him.

"Attention" he yelled, "Right turn, Forward march," he continued. They marched in line until they got to the wood. They were told to spread out and cut their way through the woods. It was difficult at first but soon they got to a clearing. They then ordered to line up and march forward. This went on for hours. It seemed like it was going on forever. It was about one when they were told to stop and rest. They all found a place to rest and sat down on the ground. It was about a half hour later that an Army truck pull up. Sergeant Halisek sat down next to Gino and Andy

"Where are we going?" asked Andy.

"We are not going anywhere," responded Sergeant Halisek. "We are on a field trip. We have walked thirty miles. We now will have lunch and head back in time for supper." Sure enough the truck delivered a hot lunch. After lunch they all marched back to the camp. They were almost too tired to eat supper. Gino and Andy sat in their bunk for about an hour before they went to the Food Court.

CHAPTER TWO

It was on the Friday, after the daily routine the sergeant call them to attention in front of the barracks.

"I want to inform you that you have the weekend off," said Sergeant Halisek. "You can travel anywhere you wish, but you have to be back by Monday morning." He then released them and left.

"Wow," said Andy. "That was unexpected."

"What are we going to do," said Gino. "We have been so active that I don't know what to do with free time."

"The other night," said Andy. "I was talking to a member of another squad. I think he was from Company C. He was from a group north of our Company. He was just wondering around to check out other areas. Since I had not seen him before, I stated to talk with him. Anyway he has been here for three months and found from other members that they could get a train to Charlotte to a USO club located there."

"That's in North Carolina," said Gino. "Isn't that pretty far away? Although I admit that I don't really know where we are. I heard that we are in South Carolina."

"We are just a few miles south of Lancaster. That's near the border to North Carolina," said Andy. "However, they have been going there ever weekend they had off."

"I'm game," said Gino," when do we leave?"

"That's the problem," said Andy. "We have to be at the train station about six tonight. We will have to eat supper at charlotte. Pack a small bag with a set of underwear and shaving equipment and get ready to go. I can get the fellow that takes guys to Lancaster to drop us off at the train station.

Everything went according as Andy was told. It took about one and a half hour to get to Charlotte. They walked about two blocks from the train station to a hotel. Fortunately they had two rooms available. They walked to a nearby restaurant and had a late supper. By the time they got back to the hotel it was after ten. Being tired they went right to bed.

The Next morning, as they had agreed, they meet at the hotel restaurant at nine. They ordered breakfast and asked the waitress where the USO club was located.

"It is about six blocks west of here on the other side of the street," said the waitress, "I understand that they open at eight in the morning and that they have movies and all kinds of games to play."

"We are more interested in music and dancing," said Gino.

"If you only want to go there to dance, the orchestra doesn't start until eight."

"Thank you," said Andy. They ate their breakfast and spent the rest of the day detouring around the city. At noon they found themselves near a city park. In the park there was a food wagon. They each had a hamburg r and continued around the city. They enjoyed the trip very much.

"You know," said Gino. "I think this trip was worth it even if the USO club isn't fun. Well it is about six; let's stop at the restaurant we went to last night. I love their food." Andy agreed so they went back as Gino requested. At about seven thirty they went to the USO Club. Inside they found several people sitting at tables that were set around the dance floor. A couple of women were clearing some tables and two women were setting up the stage for the musicians that were expected at eight. Three young girls were standing near the door talking together. One of the girls facing the door attracted Gino. She was a beautiful girl with light brown hair. Apparently she was attracted to Gino because she just stood there looked at Gino. Gino, felling awkward, walked up to her.

"Hi, said Gino. "This is the first time we are here. My name is Gino Cozano. Do we just pick a table to sit and can you tell us what is served."

"My name is Elena Grafter," she said seeming very nervous. "Yes you can sit anywhere you like. At lunch time we serve sandwiches, but after seven we only serve beer and soft drinks."

"When does the music start?" asked Andy.

"It starts at eight," answered Elena, still looking at Gino.

"Are you a waitress?" asked Gino.

"No," answered Elena with a beautiful smile on her face that excited Gino. "No we are volunteers. We are here to provide dance partners for the GI's."

"I hope you will save some dances for me," said Gino.

"You will be the first," promised Elena. Gino and Andy found an empty table and sat down. Andy noticed that there was what looked like a bar at the other end of the room. He also saw a couple of solders standing in front of it.

"I think we have to go get our own drinks," said Andy. They walked up to the bar and ordered drinks. Andy ordered a beer, and Gino ordered a soft drink. At seven the band started to play. A few minutes after the music started Elena walked up to Gino.

"Are you ready for your first dance?" she asked.

"I have never been more ready for anything," said Gino thinking it was a stupid comment. Anyway they did start dancing. Gino was thrilled to have her in his arms. She was a wonderful dancer. The next song was a waltz. Gino loved to dance waltzes. After a few steps they found that they began dancing across the room like professionals. Soon they were moving gracefully across the dance floor. A few of the people who were dancing moved to the ends of the floor and stopped to watch them. Gino never felt better. He was enjoying the feeling. He felt like he was floating in air. The next song was a slow one. They started dancing cheek to cheek. After dancing the next two songs Gino started to talk.

"I'm surprised that no one has cut in," he said. "You are so beautiful and a fantastic dancer. I'm surprised that they aren't all over you"

"Thank you," said Elena. "I think that after that fantastic waltz that we danced, the fellows are afraid that they can't live up to the standard. Besides you are the fantastic dancer. I never danced like that before. I felt like I was dancing with Fred Astaire."

"Thank you," said Gino not knowing what else to say. After a few dances while they were dancing cheek to cheek, Elena decided that they should talk.

"Gino," she started, "please tell me about your life. Where are you from? What are your plans for the future?"

"I am Italian as you can tell by my name. I was born in Cleveland Ohio, where I live now with my parents. I will be 19 in August. I have plans to go to College. I would like to become an Electronic Engineer. I don't know what else to tell you."

"Why do you choose Electronic Engineering?" asked Elena.

"I am thrilled by the technology that can send a picture through the air,"

"Do you have a girlfriend back in Cleveland that is waiting for you?" asked Elena. "I'm sorry that is none of my business."

"No" answered Gino. "I never had time for a romance. I was too busy studying. I knew if I wanted to g t the degree that I want, I have to have good grades."

"Well how did you make out?"

"I got A's in math, science and all the other subjects except history. I only got B's in history. But that is enough about me. What is your background and what is your goal for the future?"

"I don't really have much to tell you," Said Elena. "I am doing pretty well in high school. I am a senior. I will be 18 next month. I want to go to college and be a nurse. I like helping other people."

"That is a very wonderful goal," said Gino. "It tells me a lot about you"

"What does it tell you about me?" asked Elena.

"It tells me that you are a very sweet hearted person," said Gino. Then to change the subject he asked her, "Am I tying you up. Do you want to dance with other fellows?" Elena pulled him up closer to her.

"I'm happy just where I am," she said. "I could dance with another soldier next week if you're not here. Then as a second thought she asked "Am I tying you up. Perhaps you want to dance with some of the other girls."

"What other girls are you talking about?" asked Gino. "I don't see any other girl." That brought Elena a little laughter. "I think we are alone here, aren't we?" After that no one spoke. After several different types of music which they dealt with like professionals, Gino noticed that the lights over the dance floor started to flash on and off.

"I think they are telling us that the place is ready to close," said Elena. Just then the band stopped playing and started to pack up their equipment.

"I had such a wonderful time," said Gino. "I hope the next time I come you will be here."

"I'm here every Saturday," said Elena. "The next time you come, look for me. I will save you some dances. And also I had a very good time too." It was hard for Gino to say goodbye. He wondered if he would ever see her again.

After saying good bye Gino and Andy headed back to their hotel.

"I think I danced with ever girl in the USO," said Andy, "except the one you were dancing with. You really had her tied up. You didn't come to the table to finish you soda."

"She really got to me," said Gino. "Do you believe in love at first sight?"

"I didn't before but maybe I do now," said Andy. "Be careful, or you may end up with a broken heart."

"I know," said Gino, "when would I see her again. Who knows how long the war will last."

"By the way," said Andy. "While you were dancing a fellow soldier came and sat in your place. He just wanted a place to sit just long enough to drink his beer. He said he would get up as soon as you came back to your seat. Of course you never came back. What I want to tell you is that he came here at about four o'clock. There is a train that leaves about two Saturday afternoon. That would save us the cost of a night here at the hotel."

"Sounds great," said Gino. "Let's look into that. We have seen all that I want to see of the city. I would rather rest Saturday after a week of workout."

"Yes, me to," said Andy.

The training got easier every week. Soon it was too easy and got boring. They no longer got tired during the long 30 mile hikes. It was two week before Gino and Andy got to go to Charlotte. After a short dinner they went to the USO club. Elena was there waiting for him.

"Hi, she said. "I missed you last week. I guess you couldn't get off. "I know," said Gino. "They never tell us ahead of time. They tell us Friday"

"Well you're here now so let's start dancing," said Elena. "I have missed our ball room dances." It just happened, as she said that that the band started to play one of their favorite waltzes. Hearing the music they automatically went into their ball room dance. After that the band played a Polka. They didn't really like to dance to a polka.

"Let's sit this one out," suggested Elena. "Let's get a drink and sit for a while."

"Good Idea," said Gino, "The drinks are on me." Gino bought a drink for both and they sat at the table that Andy was sitting in.

"You guy don't like polkas?" asked Andy.

"It's not out style," said Elena.

"Have you met Elena?" asked Gino.

"No but I have seen her for hours here at the USO," kidded Andy.

"I'm sorry said Gino with a smile on his face. Andy I want you to meet Elena, and Elena this is Andy who is a member of the same squad as I am."

"Glad to meet you Andy," said Elena. "I see you have a sense of humor. I'm sorry that I didn't come over and say hello the last time you guys were here. I was having too much fun dancing. I don't get to dance with such a fantastic dancer very often."

"I guess I will see you the next time they play a polka," said Andy. "It may be a month from now."

"Very funny," said Elena. "Let's dance Gino. We don't want to disappoint Andy" They both got up and moved to the dance floor.

"I'm sorry that Andy was so unfriendly," said Gino. "He is really a very nice guy."

"No," said Elena. "I enjoy his sense of humor. He was just kidding us. He was right. The last time you were here we never left the dance floor." After that they danced to several new songs. Gino was so confident that they would be dancing together all night that he never expected what happen next. As they were dancing cheek to cheek to a very slow romantic song Gino felt a tap on his shoulder.

"May I cut in?" said a young man standing next to Gino. It was so unexpected that Gino let go of Elena and walked away wondering what he could have done to prevent what happened. Gino walked to the table where Andy had been sitting. Andy however was not there. He had found a girl to dance with and was at the other end of the dance floor. After the song that was playing ended, Elena pulled away from the fellow she was dancing with, said, thank you, and walked over to Gino. She had a big smile on her face.

"That was weird," she said.

"I know," said Gino. "Let's dance. I will be watching out so that it will not happen again. You wouldn't mind will you? Perhaps you want to dance with one of the other fellows."

"You know the answer to that," said Elena," We went over this last time you were here. However to make it clear to you, I danced with several fellows last week and I missed you at every dance."

"I missed you too," said Gino Before he could say anything more, Elena started to dance into ball room dance. They moved across the floor like bird on the fly. Fortunately Gino got in sync with her.

"What brought that on?" asked Gino.

"I saw that fellow that broke in before, heading to cut in again. I think that from here on we will have to show off our ball room dancing showman ship."

"Was the fellow discouraged?" asked Gino.

"Yes," said Elena. "He turned around and went back to his table."

"Why doesn't he get another girl to dance with?" said Gino. "I see a couple of pretty girls standing waiting to be asked."

"Who knows," said Elena. "He is sitting at the second table from the doorway. Let's keep an eye on him." They did watch him but he didn't make a move toward them again. They tried a few slow dances but he did not approach them.

"I guess he got the message," said Gino.

"We should still dance the ball room dance. I really enjoy it," said Elena. "Where did you learn to dance this way?"

"I guess you should know," said Gino. "In high school I was chairman of the dance committee. There was a girl named Jan that was a great dancer and she taught me to do the ball room dancing.

"I thought that there had to be an answer to your dancing," said Elena.

"But I still have to praise you," said Gino. "You came up to speed very nicely. You were certainly a big part of our success. Not to change the subject," said Gino, "but do you think the other fellows mine our taking up the floor space like this?"

"When the floor gets crowded we have to go into the regular dance routine. Besides if it is crowded we couldn't do it anyway. However, when there are not too many dancing they don't seem to mind. Look on the side lines. They are just standing there watching. I think they are enjoying the show we are putting on."

"Let's give them a long lasting thrilling show," said Gino. Gino put on some of his fancy steps. It thrilled the audience. It also thrilled Elena. She was surprised that she was able to follow every step. She also realized that Gino was pulling her into every move. The evening went by too fast. Soon Gino found himself back at the base.

The next morning when they were called to attention, Sargent Halisek informed them that they were going into a new phase in the program. Most of the new exercises place them in formations like they were attacking an invisible enemy. However they were performed at different areas. One of the interesting events was when they were directed to the firing range. First they were firing at a target with their rifle and the next day they were firing at a target with a pistol. They were graded for their performance. Gino earned a sharp shooters metal. That Friday they were told that they had performed exceptionally well and deserved a week end off. Gino and Andy didn't have to hear it twice. They made plans to be on the train on Saturday afternoon. The plan was to be in the USO club by eight.

They had dinner at their favorite place in Charlotte and went to the USO club at exactly at eight. In side Gino looked for Elena, who was always in the end of the hall waiting for him. Gino was surprised that she was not there. He looked around and found her dancing with a fellow soldier. As the music ended Elena looked towards the entrance and saw Gino. Andy had moved in a located a table. Gino had just stood at the entrance way. Elena walked over to Gino.

"Hi," she said. "What are you doing here?"

"I came to dance with you," said Gino surprised at her question.

"I know but I didn't expect you," she said. "I thought you would be here every other week end. That has been the usual thing since I've been coming here. Anyway I am so glad to see you. Let's dance before it gets crowded. They are playing our favorite waltz. "You can tell me why you are here. You are not moving out I hope." They went into their favorite dance.

"No, we are not moving that I know of," said Gino. "Although they don't tell us anything, I don't think so because they just started us on a new harder set of performance tasks. The old tasks became too easy and boring. We have built up our bodies too well. The reason I am here is that they said that we had performed exceptional well and deserved an extra week end off. Incidentally, one of the new requirements is that we learn to shoot accurately. So I have spent time on the Rifle Range and the Pistol Range. We were all tested yesterday. Guess what? I won the Sharp Shooters Medal."

"Wow," said Elena. "I did notice that you had an extra metal attached to your uniform. Congratulations"

"Thank you," said Gino. "Let's concentrate on our dancing performance. I feel extra joyful tonight." They did dance the rest of the night. Their ball room stile dancing improved with each dance. Gino had started to teach Elena special dance steps. He taught her how to let go and spin around and end up into his arms at the end of her spin. After a night of dancing they decided to sit for a while. They got so good that near the end of the day while they were having a soft drink they were asked to perform for them. They only had time for one dance when the lights started to blink. The evening ended too soon.

That week was tougher than the previous weeks. Their march through the wood was faster and longer. They ended at the other end of the woods. They slept that night in a tent. After they were given a small breakfast they were marched back to camp at a fast pace. When they got back to camp they all went right to bed. The next day they went back to the regular training. That week end was the regular week off. Andy and Gino left at the usual time Saturday. However there was an accident on one of the cross roads and the train was delayed. They arrived at the USO at about eight forty five. As they entered Gino saw Elena dancing with another soldier. Gino stood there watching them dance. Suddenly Gino saw Elena whisper in her partner's ear and walked away from him. It was in the middle of the song. She then walked up to Gino and hugged him.

"I'm so glad to see you," said Elena. "I was afraid you wouldn't make it."

"There was an accident on the tracks and our train was delayed. We didn't even have dinner."

"We can leave here and go down the street just a couple of blocks from here to a restaurant I like," said Elena. "It not only has good food but it also has a nice band."

"No," said Gino. "I can go one day without dinner." Gino wanted to ask her what she had whispered to the fellow she was dancing with, but couldn't bring himself to ask. He didn't want to put pressure on her. If she wanted to she would tell him later. They danced mostly slow romantic normal dancing. No one tried to break in.

"Elena," said Gino getting up some courag . "You know that I am very fond of you, don't you."

"Yes," she answered, "I am very fond of you too. But I don't feel this is the time to discuss this. For now let's just say that we are very good friends." They dances the rest of the night without bring up the point. Often Gino make Elena laugh with some of his funny stories of things he did as a kid. After the lights started to flash the end of the day Gino and Elena walked to the entrance way. Andy followed behind. Gino tried to kiss Elena go d night but she resisted.

"Can a friend kiss his friend good night?" asked Gino. The desire in Gino's eyes weakened her. Besides, she wanted him to kiss her as badly as Gino wanted to kiss her.

"I guess it will be all right," she said pulling him close to her. Gino didn't need to think about it. Besides he was afraid that she would change her mind if he delayed. Their lips touched gently. After a light kiss they started to part. However as they parted they looked into each other eyes and the desire overcame them. They then kissed again much more passionately. They did not part until Andy spoke up.

"We had better leave before we get shut up in here," he said. "They are starting to close the doors." They walked outside and Gino gave Elena a final good night kiss. On the way to the hotel Andy turned to Gino

"Friend, do you know what you are getting into?"

"A lot of fun," responded Gino.

"You are working your way into a severe heart break," said Andy. "Don't you see that a relationship with Elena will never work?"

"What are you talking about?" asked Gino.

"What I am saying is that we will be leaving the area in a few more days. Then you will be shipped overseas. How long will the war last? It could last several years. Then after you get discharged you will want to go to college. That will be another four or even five years. We are guessing it will be about ten years before you will be available. Think about what you are doing."

"I don't care," said Gino. "We can communicate by mail until I am available."

"Well I have given you my thoughts," said Andy. "I don't have anything else to say." They soon went into the hote and went to sleep.

The next two weeks were easier on them. Each had the weekly personal reviews but this week it was deeper than the others. It was given by Lieutenant Stillman rather than Sargent Halisek. Gino figured that it was to determine which position in the service he would be better fitted for.

"Well," said the lieutenant, "I will turn you over to your squad leader." That was a surprise to Gino. He usually went free after the review. A few minutes later Sargent Halisek walked in.

"Hi," Private Cozano," he started. "I have good news for you. You will have this weekend to celebrate you graduation from basic training. Next Friday you will be shipping out."

"Do you know where we will be going," asked Gino.

"Well first you will be going home for eight days. Instructions to where you go from there will be given you on next Friday." Saturday morning Gino looked for Andy. He was just coming back from breakfast. Gino had eaten earlier. He wanted to go to the USO early since it would be the last time they would be able to go. He was hoping to catch Elena early so they could spend more time together.

"Hi Andy," said Gino. "I was hoping that we could go early so that I could spend more time with Elena."

I'm sorry Gino," replied Andy. "I don't think I will go today."

"Why not?" asked Gino feeling disappointed. "I could use the company."

"I have no reason to go," said Andy. "I don't have any one there. Besides I have a lot of things to look over, what I want to bring home or leave here. I'm sorry. You don't need me anyway. I never see you when we are there." Gino then decided to go early. However, he missed the early train and caught the next available. That train got him to charlotte in the late afternoon. When he walked into the USO it was just after five o'clock. He was hoping that Elena was there. He was in luck. Elena was there watching two soldiers playing pink pong. She noticed Gino, gave an excuse to the two soldiers and walked up to Gino.

"Gino," she said with a wondering look on her face, "what are you doing here?"

"I wanted to spend more time with you," answered Gino.

"Oh no," said Elena. "You are not leaving are?"

"You are not stuck here for the rest of the day, are you?" asked Gino. "I was wondering if we could go someplace and talk."

"I was just getting ready to go out for supper," said Elena. "Come to think about it there is a restaurant not too far from here that has music all day. They start at lunch time and end at midnight. Let's go there, and their food is excellent."

I will go on one condition," said Gino, and that is that I pay all the bills."

"It was my idea," said Elena, "and I would have paid for my dinner anyway."

"I promised myself when I was in high school, that I would never let a date, or any girl, that I had a meal with, pay for the bill. I have kept this promise up to now. Do you want to break my record?"

"Oh God forbid," said Elena with a smile on her face. "Come it is only a short walk from here. It will increase our appetite. Since my dinner will be free I want to eat as much as I can. By the way, I knew that you would offer to pay the bill so I chose a very expensive restaurant."

"Very funny," said Gino. "After all we have to pay for the music." After walking about four blocks they came to the restaurant. It was called Bella Fontana. "That means beautiful fountain," said Gino. "Is that there main meal, water?"

"They have the biggest bar in the city," said Elena. As they entered Gino realized that Elena was joking. There in the middle of the entrance was the most beautiful fountain Gino had ever seen.

"Ha, ha," said Gino as they were led to a table. "You are a real jokester."

"Let's eat first said Elena. "I know that what you are going to tell me is going to be very sad. I don't want to spoil our dinner."

"Whatever you say," answered Gino. The waitress handed them the menu. They looked it over discussing the different choices. "They all look so good," said Gino. "Since you have apparently been here before what would you recommend?"

"It's hard for me too," said Elena. "But I had lamb chops here and they were fantastic. They were real lamb Chops, not like some place that serves lamb chops that look like miniature T-b ne steaks."

"That sounds great to me," said Gino. "I know what you mean. I have never been able to order true lamb chops in Ohio either. I always had to buy the lamb ribs, cut them into chops and cook them myself." When the waitress returned they ordered the chops.

"Let's dance while we wait for our food," suggested Elena. "I would like to feel your arms around me." Gino was not asked twice. They danced cheek to cheek for several songs.

"I am going to miss this," said Gino.

"Let's not start talking about that," said Elena. "Let's enjoy the moment. We will talk later." Gino squeezed Elena hard against his body. He realized that she was right. He had to enjoy the moment.

Elena realized that Gino had squeezed her harder. She turned her head slightly and kissed Gino on his cheek. They continued dancing until Gino noticed that the waitress had placed their food on the table.

"We had better go and eat our dinner," said Gino. "We don't want it to get cold." They sat and eat there Lamb chops. While they were eating they each told each other what their dreams were.

"I wish that I will settle down to a nice house," said Elena finishing her dream desires, "with a romantic man that loves me and I would love to raise four children."

"That is a beautiful goal," said Gino. "I would like the same thing except I would like to be an electronic engineer as I have told you before." After they finished eating, they both looked like they didn't want dinner to be over.

"Before we start talking let's dance," said Elena. "They are playing one of our favorite songs." They started to dance but Gino could not keep from talking.

"Elena," he started. "I don't want to lose you. We have to think of a way that we could stay together?"

"I guess you want to get it over with," said Elena. "Let's sit down with a cup of coffee and discuss it." They went to the table and ordered a cup of coffee.

"I don't know where they will send me," said Gino, "and how long the war will last but we have to be ready for it."

"What do you mean to be ready?" asked Elena.

"Well, let's say the war gets over this year," said Gino. "We can then get together."

"Yes but what if the war lasts three or four years," said Elena. "Besides don't you want to go to colleg ? Even if the war only lasts two years, and you add four years for colleg , and then you have to work at least two years to be able to support a wife, and come back here, After all you live on the other side of the nation. We are talking about ten years that we would be apart.

"Let's get down to the bottom line," said Gino. "What I am asking you, is for your address so that we could write to each other and decide after we know what was happening."

"Look Gino," said Elena. "I am a teenager in high school. I admit it, I am very much in love with you, but I don't want to hang all my dreams on a maybe. Then, if five years from now you forget about me find another girl in college or in your town, and drop me, I will have dreams destroyed and I will live with an incurable broken heart."

"Aren't you thinking of the worst case?" said Gino.

"No," Gino, said Elena. "I know what time does. I have only seen you four times. My heart will be broken when you leave. But later it will be like a wonderful dream. It will heal in a few days. I admit that the USO would bring back my thoughts of you. I may not go back there for several months. But your leaving is not unexpected. It is no surprise. I have expected it since we met. I can get over it now. I would have a hard time getting over it four years from now."

"Are you saying that this is goodbye?" asked Gino with small tears in his eyes.

"No," said Elena, "you have my last name. If things turn out that I am the love of your life and you find that you can't live without me you can come and find me."

"I do love you very much. So can you imagine my heart break if you are married when I find you?" said Gino.

"So you do love me," said Elena with a smile. "Do you know that this is the first time that I could remember that you told me that? Anyway, I will not be married for a long time. I want to go to college too, remember. I will probably be a nurse. As you can tell I like to help people. If my grades are good I may continue on to school to be a doctor. So if you wait that long, you will not remember me anyway."

"Let's stop all this heart breaking discussion," said Gino. "Let's dance until they close. I want my arms around you as long as I can." They danced the rest of the evening. To Gino it went to fast. Soon they were told that they were closing. Gino looked Elena in the eyes. He saw small tears beginning to show. He didn't hesitate to take advantage of the moment. He would never have another chance. He kissed her lightly on the lips. Suddenly it turned into a hard pressed kiss. The closing announcement was again repeated. Gino and Elena slowly left the restaurant.

"I'll walk you to your hotel," said Elena. "It is on my way back to the USO club. My car is parked in its parking lot." There was nothing said as they walked to the hotel. As they stopped at the entrance way Gino wrapped his arms around her and gave her a passionate kiss. He knew that it would be the last one. Elena did not resist. She wrapped her arms tightly around his neck. After a few minutes their tongues began to search for each other. After their passion rose to a level too high for Elena to continue, she pulled herself away from Gino. She looked straight into his eyes for a minute as if to take a last look. Then she stepped back

"Good bye Gino." She said. "I will always remember these last months and I will always love you." With that she turned around and walked away. Gino watched her walk down the street into the darkness and disappear.

The trip back was later than he had hoped for. The next train available was after twelve midnight. He got to bed it was about a quarter to three. It was hard for him to be up and in line at the call of the bugle. Fortunately the week was not a rough one. They spent most of the time reviewing the operation and firing of anti-aircraft guns. They reviewed the calculating of the height of the aircraft so that they will know how advanced to the aircraft they had to aim so that the missile would get at the same point at the same time as the aircraft. The rest of the week was also a review of all that they had learned during their stay at the camp. That Friday after the morning line up they were marched to a troop truck and shipped to the train station. Gino was surprised at the number of soldiers that were at the train station ready to travel on the same train as some of his squad members were. Gino and Andy were led to the last car of the train. After the train left the station Andy turned to Gino.

"Grab your duffle bag and come with me," he said. "We should do this before someone else decides to do it."

"What are you talking about?" asked Gino.

"Just grab your bag and come with me," repeated Andy. Gino did as Andy requested and followed him to the far end of the train. When they got there Andy opened the doors and stepped out onto the little open terrace like area. He sat his Duffle bag next to the railing that surrounded the area and sat down.

"What are we doing here?" asked Gino surprised at Andy's action.

"Set your bag here next to mine and sit here," said Andy. "We can sit here and watch the scenery during the whole trip. It is nice and cool here. We don't want to sit inside in the hot car."

"Why not?" said Gino as he set his duffle bag next to Andy and sat down. "It is a softer seat and your right it is a lot cooler here." As they were sitting there they were surprised that as they travel through the farm land that the farmers working their land would stop working and wave to them. They of course waved back. It gave them a sense of being appreciated. It was great. About an hour later as they traveled through a city they got another joyful surprise. As the train slowed down, the people who were standing on the street side walk would also wave at them.

"The people are so friendly. I think they appreciate what we are doing for the freedom of America," said Gino.

"Yes," added Andy. "I think they are kind of saying thank you." This continued for hours as they traveled north. The only time that Gino felt bad was when the traveled through the city of Charlotte. Gino was hoping that he would somehow see Elena on the road. He however knew that it would have been a miracle. As they traveled the eight hour trip to Cleveland, they noticed something they had never expected. Andy brought it up first.

"Have you notice?" said Andy, "that as we travel through Virginia some of the farmers wave and only half of the pedestrians wave. The farther north we go the fewer people seem to notice us." From there to Ohio they noticed that fewer and fewer people waved at them. When they got to Columbus, they notice, as they traveled through the city that no one waved at them. In fact, one woman looked behind her wondering who they were waving at. Another woman looked at them with a big frown of wonderment on her face. The men didn't even look up. It was that way the rest of the way to Cleveland.

"I don't understand," said Gino. "Are the people up north less friendly then the people down south?"

"I think that they are more busy here then the people down south," said Andy. "Most work in factories and other hard working jobs."

"They also have factories down south," said Gino, "and I don't think anyone works longer and harder than the farmers."

"All I can say," said Andy, "is that they are different societies."

When they got near to Cleveland Gino became curious.

"Andy," Gino asked. "Are you going all the way to Cleveland?"

"Yes," said Andy. "I will take a different train from Cleveland to Pittsburg." When they got to Cleveland, Gino and Andy stopped at the center of the train station.

"Well this is where we part," said Andy. "I am going to see what is available to take me east."

"I see a taxi cab at the curb," said Gino. "Since we are part of the same squad, I think I will see each other in eight days."

"Take care," said Andy as he walked away. Gino went out, got the cab and headed for home. When he got there it was about five. As he got out of the cab, Gino's sister saw the cab and came out shouting.

"Mom, Gino is home." As she got to the curb she threw herself into his arms. "Hi big brother," she said "It's so good to see you. We all missed you."

"Hi Mary," said Gino. How is my baby sister?" She never got to answer because Gino's mother threw her arms around him.

"Gino," she started. "I've worried about you every day. How are you?" "I'm fine mother," answered Gino. "I'm glad to be home even if it will be for a short time."

"Well you have come home just at the right time," said Gino's mother. "I don't know if it was a foresight, but I just cooked your favorite dinner. I cooked Cavatelli with pork neck bones that you love." Gino didn't have to be told twice. He pulled his duffle bag into the entrance way and proceeded to the kitchen table. Gino's mother added another setting and proceeded to provide dinner.

"Well Gino," asked his mother. "How long are you going to be with us?

"I will be home for eight days. I have to be in Detroit by eight Monday morning.

"That is not very long," said Gino's mother looking very sad. "I do have bad news. We didn't want to tell my mail But Uncle Joe got a job in Arizona. They moved there last week. I was hoping that you would come home before they left"

"Tell us about your experience at the army camp," asked his sister Mary. "What did you do over the four months that you were gone?" Gino tried to explain all the exercises that he went through day by day. The repeated schooling on the operations of the anti-air-craft equipment seemed to interest his father.

"All the other things that you did, it is obvious was to strengthen your body," said Gino's Father. "However the instruction on the anti-aircraft equipment is different. Do you think they were preparing you for that type of service?"

"I don't know dad. I will not know until I report to the Army deployment office in Detroit." The rest of the evening they just spent on small talk.

The eight days went by too fast. They spent the time together. They didn't even want to watch TV. On Monday Gino's mother gave Gino a Going away present. She gave him a small camera.

"I want you to take picture," she said, "of all the places you are going to be shipped. And if possible send me copies."

"I have no idea if that will be possible. However, if I can't get them develop, I will take pictures when possible and I will bring them home when I am discharged. On Wednesday afternoon while Gino was sitting on the porch he noticed Carmela, the girl next door. She was about ten years older than Gino. She had enlisted in the navy just after the war started.

"Hi Carmela," said Gino. "How are you? I see you got a leave at the same time as I did. Where are you stationed and what do you do there?" She told him that she was stationed at a naval station in New York. She tried to explain what her duties were and Gino acted like he understood however he got lost in the center of her description. She also told him that she was leaving the next day

"Say, while we are here together," said Gino. "I would like to take a picture of us both in uniform. It will be a remembrance of this day."

"Sure why not," said Carmela. "Make sure you give me a copy whenever you can. Perhaps it will not b possible until we are both discharged." Gino called his mother who took a picture of the both together. After a few minutes they both wish each other good luck and parted.

Sunday after Church Gino prepared to depart. He packed his duffle bag and when time came to leave they all were showing the sadness that they felt. The sorrow that they felt was worse than the first time he left. That time they were in a trance and didn't realize he would be gone so long. He kissed every one and forcing himself from his mother's arms. He tearfully left for the train station.

CHAPTER THREE

On to the War Zone

Gino stepped into the army office in Detroit at five minutes to eight. He was surprised that the office was full of soldiers waiting to be assigned. New soldiers were entering behind him by the dozen. He was standing there waiting for directions when he heard a voice behind him call out his name. He turned around.

"Andy" he yelled out. "It is so goo to see you. I guess we are both part of the same squad." Gino put out his hand but Andy grabbed Gino and gave him a big hug.

"Good to see you too," said Andy. Before they could say anything more a door at the other end of the room opened and a corporal started to call out names. Gino's name was the third name called. He was led through the door to another large room. About two dozen other names were called. Fortunately Andy's name was one of the ones called. After calling out the last name the corporal closed the door and walk up to the desk at the end of the room.

"Hello fellow members of the USA military force. My name is Corporal Linski. I am the temporary guide to your next stop. You are all members of The US army company D. You are now reassigned and transferred as members of the 743rd AAA Gun Battalion. If you all will follow me I will deliver you to the train station for your travel to your next Army Base." With that said he brought them to troop carrier trucks and drove them to the train station. They were then lead to a train car that was set up just for them. As they got on board one of the men stopped and turned to the corporal.

"Can you give us an Idea as to where we are being shipped to," he asked

"I'm sorry," said the corporal. "Didn't I tell you where you were going? Well, you are being shipped to the army base in San Francisco."

"I hope we will stay there to protect the US," said Andy.

"It would be nice but my guess is that we are going there to be shipped overseas," said Gino.

Gino and several other soldiers were boarded on one of the train cars. It looked like at least three train cars were reserved for the army transportation. Gino and Andy were boarded on the second car from the rear. After about a half hour the train started to move. Soon it was out of the city and it went on to full speed. Andy and Gino sat together.

"I'm so glad that you are here with me," said Gino. "Having a friend with you among so many unknown people and not knowing where you were going gives us a kind of comfort."

"I know, said Andy. "It's like having company on a bad trip." As the train gained full speed, Gino and Andy spent the next few hours talking about their teen age lives. At about noon they walked to the forth car which was the cafeteria. They ordered lunch and sat there after they were finished eating. It was more comfortable siting there. After a few minutes Andy noticed that two solders across from them took out a deck of cards and began playing. Andy got up and walked over to them.

"Hiya fellows," said Andy. "Would you guys mind if my friend and I joined you?"

"No, that would be great," said one of the men sitting there. "That would be perfect." Andy then called Gino and the all sat together.

"My name is Andy and my friend here is Gino."

"I'm Fred and this is Paul," said Fred pointing to his buddy. They all shook hands. They played several different games. They all seemed to like Poker. They only bet one dollar as the highest bid. The next game they liked was Uno. They changed often and the day went by joyfully. It was during the second day that after eating lunch they hear music coming from the next care past the cafeteria car. They walked to where the music came from. As they entered the car they saw about seven solders, some sitting and some standing around two others, one with a mouth organ and the other with a small guitar. They were all singing familiar songs. One of the songs was a Christmas song. When the song was over Andy walked over to the one that looked like the leader.

"That is so wonderful to spent the times singing, said Andy. However I wonder why you are singing Christmas songs? Christmas is about two months away."

"I know," said the leader. "We are just now getting to know each other. We never met before we got on the train. So being strangers the only songs we know together are Christmas songs."

"So you mind if we join you?" asked Gino.

"No," said a few in unison.

"The more the merrier," said another of the group. They all sang the rest of the afternoon. They found some non-Christmas songs that a few knew. They sang those as often as someone suggested one. At supper time they all moved on into the cafeteria. After dinner Andy and Gino moved back to their seats to rest. Gino had brought a small paperback book and sat down to read.

During the next day they played cards for about an hour, sat and listen to the music for about an hour and then went back to their seats for the rest of the trip. Later that day they were asked to eat their dinner at five because the train would reach its destination about six-thirty. Right on time the train pulled into the San Francisco station at six-thirty. They were lead to an Army Troop truck and shipped to the Amy base. When they got there they were assign a barracks to settle in. When they entered the barracks Andy and Gino where shocked. Sargent Halisek and the rest of the squad were settling in also. After a small conversation Gino and Andy realized that the other three squads were also there. Also they were told that all of Company D would eventually come together there.

The next morning, Sargent Halisek called them together in front of the barracks.

"It will be a couple of days before the complete company will be assembled to be shipped overseas," informed the Sargent. "So in the mean time you are all free to wander down to the city. Don't go too far and make sure you come back to your barrack every night. We will assemble every morning and I will inform you of your next move."

"I understand that there is a USO club nearby," asked Andy. "Is it close, and are we allowed going there?"

"Yes to both of your questions," said the Sargent. "If you walk east of the barracks you will find a country road that leads down the mountain side. If you walk down that road it will lead you to the main street of a small suburb. Walk west on the main road and you will come to the USO club. It will be on your right. However it will take over an hour to walk down. So make sure you provide enough time to get back before it gets to dark and you will get lost."

"Thank you sir," said Andy. The next day Andy and Gino decided to take the trip. After lunch they left following the Sarg nt directions. The Army base was up on a hill, so the walk was all downhill. When they were about fifteen minutes on the road, Gino turned to Andy.

"Well Andy," started Gino. "What are we going to talk about as we go down the hill? Do you have a go d story to tell me?"

"Have you heard the story of Phil Philaphanusa?" asked Andy.

"Phil pha… who," asked Gino. "I never hear of him. Who is he?"

"Phil was a soldier in the World War 1 Army," started Andy. "When the war was over he got his discharge in France. He spent the next year roaming around Paris. One day he got a letter from the mayor of Paris. On the envelope it stated that he had to report to the French office for Alien Affairs. It gave him the address. So the next day he followed the instruction and reported as requested. When he got there he was lead to the main office. Sitting at the desk was a high level officer of the French Army. The officer stated that he understood that Phil had been given a letter from the Mayor of Paris. The officer asked Phil to give him the letter. He told Phil that it had been given to him by mistake. It was supposed to be giving directly to him. Phil handed him the letter. As he read the letter you would have thought that he went mad. He raised his voice and yelled in French and finally called for the Sargent that had led him into the office. He yelled to him in French giving him directions. He threw the letter at Phil. Phil was free enough to place the letter into his pocket. The Sargent took out hand cuffs and hand cuffed Phil and grabbed him by the arm and started to pull him out of the office. Phil asked him to explain what was going on. The office told him that he was unworthy to stay in France and was to be taken to the border and not allowed to enter into France again. The Sargent place Phil in an army car and drove him to the German border. At the German boarder they let him in but he was asked to wait awhile before going into the nearby town. A border officer called his superior. A few minutes later a high class looking gentleman showed up. The fellow said that he understood that France has asked him to leave France. He wanted to know why. Phil told him that he really didn't know. He told him that he got this letter and after a French officer read it he had him escorted out of the country. Phil told him that he didn't even tell him what he had done that was wrong. The man asked him if he still had the letter. Phil gave the letter to the man. The man read it and told the officer in German language to escort the man to the Italian boarder. Phil did not understand German so he asked what was going on."

"Wait a minute," interrupted Gino, "when are you going to end this story" We are almost to the city. Just tell me what was in the letter."

"I'm almost done," said Andy. "Have a little patience."

"You have been telling this story for nearly an hour. Cut it short."

"Ok," said Andy. "The man told him that he was not allowed to be in Germany and was being lead to the Italian border. To make the story shot, the same thing happen at the Italian boarder. Phil then asked to be brought to the airport and go a ticket to the USA. He was sure that his own country would not kick him out. However, he decided to keep the letter from any American official. When he got to New York he remembered that he had a brother that understood French that lived in New York. So before getting a ticket to his home in Ohio he called his brother and asked him to meet him at an exclusive place where they could be alone. His brother told him that the pier where his boat was docked was very free of people at midnight. So they decided to meet on the pier at midnight. When they met Phil gave his brother the letter. It was too dark for his brother to read the letter so he walked down the pier to where there was a small light. As Phil's brother walked toward the light there was a box that someone left on the pier. In the dark Phil's brother did not see it. He tripped on it and fell into the water. He had to swim to the end of the pier near the shore where there was a ladder that he could climb back up on. As he came out of the water Phil noticed that his brother still had the letter in his hand. They walked to the shore end of the pier. There they went under a street light. Phil's brother then raised the letter under the light and was amazed. The ink on the letter was all washed away. The letter was a blank piece of paper."

"Well," said Gino. "What was written on the letter?"

"I don't know," said Andy. "The writing was all washed away. No one ever found out what was written on the letter."

"You rotten dog," said Gino. "It was all a dirty joke. There never was a letter was there?"

"It did take up the time," said Andy. "You see there on the right is the sign that says USO Club. We are already here."

"It was still a lousy way to spend the time," said Gino. "I don't think I can forgive you soon."

"I'll make it up to you somehow," said Andy. "However you have a good story to tell someone."

"He would have to be a very bad enemy," said Gino. At that they both broke out in laughter.

As they entered the USO Club they noticed that most of the guests in the place were navy personnel. Most of them were just sailors on shore leave. There were no tables available so they separated. Andy went to the bar and Gino walked around looking for someone to dance with. He did find a young girl who had just sat down at a table with a soft drink. Gino walked up to her.

"Would you like to dance," he asked her.

"I would love to," said the young girl. She got up and they started to dance.

"My name is Gino," he said trying to start a conversation.

"My name Lisa," said the girl. "It's a good change to dance with a soldier," she said. "As you can see the guest here are mostly Navy men. Are you stationed here?"

"My name is Gino. I don't think so. We just go here. I think we will be sent overseas in a couple of days. How about you, do you come here often?"

"I volunteer a few days a week," said Lisa. "Most of the time it is not this busy. Although they are always mostly navy men, today is special. You see today we have a couple of movie stars here. It happens once in a while when they have just finish a movie. See if you can get to dance with one of them. It would be something you could tell your kids and grandkids."

"Do you know who they are," asked Gino getting interested.

"No not today yet," said Lisa. "I will find out later before the joint closes." After he danced a couple of dances with Lisa Gino walked around trying to find the movie stars. After about an hour he recognized two of the dancers. He recognized them from the movies he had seen before he was drafted. He couldn't remember their real names. He remembered their movie names. Suddenly he saw that one of the stars was walking away from her partner. Gino jumped at the chance and asked her to dance. She accepted.

"My name is Gino," he started. "I'm here temporarily. I think that in a few days I will be shipped overseas."

"It is nice to meet you," said the star. "My name is Betty. I just finish filming a war movie."

I know," said Gino. "I remember seeing a couple of your movies. You are one of my favorite stars."

"It's nice to meet one of my admirers." Before they could say another word Gino felt a tap on his shoulder. A sailor was cutting in. Gino walked away sadly. Then having second thought decided that if someone could cut in on him he should be able to cut in on someone. He looked around until he saw the other movie star that he recognized. With sudden buildup of courage he walked up and cut in on a sailor dancing with her. It just happened that as he tapped him on the shoulder the song ended. Gino then started to dance with her from the start of a new song.

"My name is Gino. I hope you don't mind my cutting in."

"No," she said. "I'm glad you did. He was a lousy dancer. I notice already that you are a very good dancer. I was about to leave anyway. It is getting late and I have a long way to go. By the way, my name is Rita."

"I'm glad to meet you Rita. I have been trying to dance with you all evening. I recognize you from your movies. It will be a story I could tell my children and grandchildren."

"Are you married with children?" asked Rita.

"No I'm single but I was talking about the future. I will never forget that I danced with a Movie Star called Rita. He never got to finish his statement when a sailor tapped him on the shoulder. Disgusted Gino looked for Andy. He found Andy sitting with a girl at a table. As Gino walked up to them the girl got up to leave.

"Andy, thank you for the soda and the wonderful time we had dancing. I will never forget you. I will pray daily for all of you soldiers."

"Thank you for the wonderful time I had with you," said Andy. "God bless you for all that you are giving for your country." With that said she left.

"Andy, I have had enough," said Gino. "What do you say we leave? I see your beautiful partner has left. It is almost five. What do you say we leave and stop at that restaurant we passed on the way here? I'm tired of Army food."

"Sounds like a great Idea," said Andy. "We should go back to the barracks while there is still light. I don't think we should try to find it in the dark." They left and stopped at the restaurant as planned. With a short wait they were seated. They were the only army persons there. Half were civilians and the rest were Navy men. After they ordered their meal Gino turned to Andy.

"I think this was an unforgettable evening," said Gino. "I can tell my friends and my family someday. I only wish that I knew their names. I can only remember their movie character names."

"I hear some say that the one you danced with first was call Betty Grable," said Andy. "I also think the other one there was Rita Hayworth or something like that."

I'll pretend that I hear it from them," said Gino. At that they both laughed. The only thing I regret is that I didn't bring my camera. I would have been proof of who I danced with. They ate quickly and left for the Army Base. The trip going back was harder than the way down. The trip up was all up hill. When they got to the base they were both very tired, so they both went immediately to bed.

The next morning they were asked to quickly assemble in front of their barracks. They were told to go back inside and pack all their belonging and be ready to travel. After ten minutes, Sargent Halisek called his squad to attention and marched them to a waiting truck. There were several trucks there waiting for the soldiers.

"Apparently the whole Battalion is going somewhere," said Gino.

"I hope it is somewhere in the US," said Andy. One of the other soldier they knew as Paul turned to them.

"Haven't you hear the latest news," said Paul. "You guys took off somewhere. We here had a meeting and were told of the current goings on."

"What have we missed?" asked Andy.

"First of all, have you heard that the US Air force has delivered an Atomic bomb on Japan destroying a complete city? Secondly they say that Japanese leaders and General Eisenhower have declared a cease fire and are meeting to negotiate a peace treaty. We are going to the Philippines as Occupational forces.

"I hope that means that we will not see any military action," said Gino.

"We could get some cleanup work," said Andy. "After all, the cease fire is only a few days old and we don't know the results of the negotiations."

After about a little over an hour they reached the port that was on the eastern side of the San Francisco Bay. They were soon led aboard a small Army troop ship. They were given rooms below deck. Andy and Gino managed to get the same room. There were four bunks in each room. Gino and Andy had two other roommates. They introduced each other. The other room mates were John and Albert. About an hour later they were notified through the ships speaker system that dinner was being served in the dining room that was in the center of the lower deck. Gino and Andy went but Gino was not too hungry. He just had a salad. Andy and the others ate full meals. Gino did not realize what a blessing that was.

It was early in the morning when everything went wild. It so happened that the ship left port sometime after they went to bed. Early in the morning Gino woke up due to very heavy movements of the ship. It seemed that the ship was rapidly going up and down and from side to side. The movement was getting to the boys balancing system. Andy had tried to get up and found that he felt sick to the stomach and went back to bed. Gino got up and after feeling like he wanted to vomit he decided to go up and get some fresh air. He realized that what he was feeling was sea sickness. The ships motions were making all ship members that were not used to sailing sea sick. Just as Gino reached the upper deck an announcement came over the loud speaker. They were told not to go on deck because the waves were very great and they could be washed overboard. Gino ignored the announcement. He felt like throwing up and didn't want to do in anywhere on the ship. He got to the deck and held on to the ships railing. He didn't care if the waves got him wet. If he had to throw up he wanted it to be overboard. The throw up heaves came to him but nothing came up. He felt the heaves several times but nothing came up. Gino realized that he didn't have anything to throw up since he didn't have much for dinner. As he moved up and down the deck looking for a place where the movement was not as sever he found that the softer motions in the center of the ship was affected him worse than the large movements. Somehow his body could tolerate the larger motions b tter than the slow almost undetected motions in the center of the ship. Gino held on to the railing and moved slowly always holding on to the railing. The waves were not as bad as the enouncement had said. However Gino's trousers were very wet from the waves that washed on to the deck. Gino slowly moved toward the bow of the ship. He was amazed how the bow would dip under the water and then rise up almost out of the water. After about an hour Gino decided to go back to his room and see how Andy was doing. When he got there Andy was still in bed moaning. He had thrown up into a waste basket he had found. Gino remembered that he had brought two novels that he would read when he had nothing else to do. He had forgotten all about the novels. He had never had a time with nothing to do. He got one out of his duffel bag and started to read it, but gave up when looking at the pages caused him to feel dizzy. He climbed into his bed to relax for a while. He could see why Andy felt better in bed. He fell asleep. After about an hour he woke up. He had to relieve himself. He only had to empty his bladder. He walked up to the lavatory which was in the bow of the ship. As he walked in he hesitated from going in. On the floor in front of him were three men laying on the floor in their vomit. Gino felt like throwing up. He left as fast as he could and proceeded to the deck. He then relieved himself through the railing into the ocean.

The problem of traveling on rough waters lasted over two days. Gino and Andy had no sense of where they were. Were they in the San Francisco bay or out in the ocean? Even after the waters became calmer, Gino spent most of his time on the deck to get fresh air. It was the third day in the evening that Gino and Andy got back together.

"I'm very hungry," said Andy. "How about you, do you think that we can take a chance and get something to eat?"

"I think we should if we want to live," answered Gino. They both went to the dining room. There were about a dozen other men there. After ordering a light dinner they both sat and talked about the last three days.

"The last few days have been the worst days of my live," said Andy. "I don't remember being so sick even when I had the flu."

"I know," said Gino. "However, I feel lucky when I think of those poor guys I saw in the lavatory that is in the ship's bow."

"What happened in the bow," asked Andy. Gino explained what he saw when he entered the lavatory. "Stop, don't te l me any-more" said Andy. "You will make me sick again."

"Anyway, what I wanted to tell you is that although I felt sick I never threw up," explained Gino. "By the way did you notice the device on the wall up front of the room? It gives the day and the time of day. It says that it is Wednesday and it is five o'clock."

"I know," said Andy. "It is so big. It almost fills the top half of the wall."

"That is strange," said Gino. "My watch says that it is seven o'clock. Did they make a mistake?"

"No" said Andy. "Don't you understand? It is your watch that is wrong. Don't forget that we are traveling west. The time is earlier in the west then it is in the east. As we travel west we travel into a different time zone."

"Yes," said Gino. "I remember now. California is always three hours earlier then our time in Ohio."

"After we eat I suggest that we go back to our room," said Andy. The ships staff is all over the place cleaning up after the mess we made. I would like to get away from it all."

"I know what you mean," said Gino. "I take it you don't want to stay here. I see that some fellows are starting to play cards at the other end of the room."

"No" said Andy. "I don't feel like playing cards. How about you what have you in mind?"

"I have those novels I brought with me I think I will go into our room and read."

It was several days later that Andy and Gino were in the dining room. They had been in the dining room three times a day since they started to feed themselves. They never paid attention to the clock on the wall. This day was different. Gino noticed the clock.

"Look Andy," said Gino. "The clock says that it is Thursday three o'clock. My watch says that it is six o'clock. We must be about as far from California as California is from Ohio. That is a three hour difference."

"I think it is going to be a lot more than that, when we get to where we are going." It was the next morning when Andy and Gino went to breakfast that Gino stopped in his track.

"Look Andy," he said in awe. "The clock on the wall says it is Thursday morning."

"That is right," said Andy. "We are g ing to have two Thursday on this trip. On the way back we will probably go from Wednesday to Friday. We will not have a Thursday."

The days went by slowly. Andy and Gino lost track of time. They had no idea how long they had been on the ship. Gino got tired of reading and he and Andy spent a lot of time on the deck. It was on one of these days that Andy noticed a change in the ships direction.

"Look Gino," said Andy. The sun is now on our left. That means that the ship is headed south."

"I see why," said Gino. "Look out to the west. There seems to be some land out there. I think we are going around it. I would guess it is one of the islands of the Pacific. I would guess it is one of the Philippine islands."

"I know the Philippines real well," said Andy. "Geography was my favorite subject. I dreamed of coming here. Not under these conditions however. I think that the island that we are passing is called; I think if I remember right, Naga or something like that. As we get closer we should see a volcano. There," He said pointing out to the land getting very excited. "It's the Mayon Volcano." As they sailed past the land they could see the volcano clearly. It was releasing a small column of smoke into the air. "Now watch Gino, we will go south for a little while until we see land on both sides. Then after a while we will turn and travel North West." About an hour later as Andy had said they sailed through a gap between two islands. Soon after the ship turned and started to travel North West.

"I guess you really know this part of the world," said Gino.

"I wish I could remember more of what is coming ahead," said Andy. "I never dreamed that I would be coming here." After traveling for a couple of hours they again came to an area where they were passing a narrow stipe of water between two areas of land. Andy wasn't sure whether they were islands.

"I'm not sure of where we are," said Andy. "If I was to guess I think that to our right is the island of Mindoro and on our right is the main land of Luzon."

"Where does that put us?" said Gino being lost by Andy's remarks.

"I think we are headed towards Manila bay," said Andy. "I think we will dock at the port of the city of Manila."

"That makes me feel kind of nervous," said Gino.

"Why are you nervous?" asked Andy.

"I feel like we are about to enter the war zone," said Gino.

"Well," said Andy, "just keep in mind that the war is just about to be over."

"It's never over until it is over," said Gino. The ship traveled for about another hour. They entered an area which was very strange to Gino. "It looked like we are out in the open sea but I can faintly see land on both sides of the ship," continued Gino.

"I think we are in the middle of the Manila Bay," said Andy. "I think we will b docking soon."

"It's very funny," said Gino." On the one hand I'm looking forward to it happening and on the other hand I'm scared to death."

"I know exactly what you are feeling," said Andy. "I kind of feel the same way except I would like it to be over with. Once we get on land we will feel better."

"Let's go to lunch," said Gino. "We don't know when we will get there." After they ate lunch they came back on deck.

About an hour later the ship slowly moved into port. After it settled in port and all the port functions were completed an announcement can over the loud speaker. It requested that all men were to collect all their belongings and meet on deck by their squad leader. Andy and Gino had already loaded all their belongings in their duffle bag, so they only had to go to their room to retrieved their belongings and report back on deck. They found where Sargent Halisek was standing and got in line with the other members. They noticed that the squads were lined up in a special order.

"I think that the squads are lined up so that the companies are together," said Andy.

"It looks like there is more than one company here," said Gino. "I bet that the whole battalion is on this ship." After all were lined up, the order was given to disembark by squads. Company D was called to disembark first. Andy and Gino's squad was the first squad called to disembark. As Andy and Gino stepped on shore they were met by two young women dressed in beautiful blue uniforms. They handed each soldier a can of soda as they reached land. Andy and Gino accepted a can each and continued down where Sargent Halisek was gathering his team.

"Who were those lovely ladies?" asked Gino.

"I think they are either American Red Cross or Salvation Army volunteers," said Andy. Lead by Lieutenant Bogan the company was marched south across a field. The land was slightly elevated. After marching for about three to four miles they reach the top of the hill where they saw a large row of barracks. Just before they reached the Barracks, Andy poked Gino.

"I don't know if it makes a difference as to who the ladies are that served us the soda," said Andy, as he pointed across the field. "The sign on that building reads, American Red Cross." After reaching the barracks area each squad was assigned a barrack. After a sort speech the Lieutenant gave up control to the Squad leaders. Sargent Halisek pulled his members aside.

"I think we will only be here about two or three days. We have four companies here in this area. Each company will be assigned a different task. In the meantime, you will be on your own, but assemble here ever morning for further information. If you look to the left of the barrack just down the hill you will see a small building with a large screen that is indented about three feet across the front of the building. There will be a movie shown every night. You may go to attend that anytime while you are here. Whatever you decide, don't wander very far." He then dismissed them. Andy and Gino went in, selected a bunk and settled in. Later that day they went down and enjoyed a movie.

The next day, hearing the wakeup call, they met in front of the barracks. Sargent Halisek informed them that there was nothing new and dismissed them. Andy and Gino hung around the barracks and later joined a couple of other members of their squad and played cards. That evening Andy and Gino went down to see a movie. When they got there they were disappointed. They were playing the same movie as they did the day before. Even though they thought it was a good movie they didn't want to see it again. They returned to the barracks and shot the bull with the other members.

The next morning the whole company was called to stand at attention. A few minutes later Captain Bogan took over and called everyone to attention.

"All of Company D is being called to active duty," said the Captain. "First of all, let me inform you that an agreement has been reached between the U.S. and Japan. Japan has surrendered to our forces. However, there are a few locations where the Japanese forces have not been told, don't want to give up, or don't believe the news. All the other companies and company D, except for Platoon 106 are being shipped to northern Luzon. There is still heavy fighting going on there. There is a group of Japanese that joined a Philippine tribe that is a revolting against the Philippine government and the U.S. Platoon 106 however, will be shipped to the island of Corregidor. There is a Japanese force there that will not surrender. All members of Platoon 106 get all of your battle gear. Leave your other belongings here. You will be coming back here after the job is completed." He then commanded each platoon officer take control of his Platoon. There were two platoons in company D. Lieutenant Stillman was in charge of Platoon 106. That was the platoon that Andy and Gino's squad was in. The lieutenant calls them to order and lined them up in rows of two and marched them towards the Manila Bay. They got there about nine o'clock. There were four small boats waiting there. Two squads were loaded in each craft.

"This looks like we are on a Landing Craft," said Andy. "I have seen these in the movies."

"What are landing Crafts?" asked Gino being completely lost in the term. "Isn't a Landing Craft an airplane?"

"I'm not sure of the name," said Andy. "But this type of a boat is used to quickly land on enemy territory when they are invading the land. Notice that the front the boat is not pointed like most boats. That is because when the boat gets to the land the front of the boat opens and provides a ramp to walk down."

"Wow," said Gino. "Are we invading the island?"

"I suppose that we should be ready if the Japanese are trying to stop us from coming on land." It was about an hour later that they approached Corregidor. Both Andy and Gino were amazed at all the sunken ships they saw near the island. On some of them they could only see the smoke stacks. Some they could only see the forward guns the smoke stacks being blown away. When they got on shore there was no one there to meet them. The front of the b at did open up and provided a ramp that was about five feet wide. All four boats arrived within minutes of each other. Gino could see what an advantage an invading army would have had. They all walked out on the beach and then were marched up to the land ab ut two hundred feet from the beach. On the left of the land they could see a small hill and flat land. On the right they could see a large mountain. Just on the right at the end of the mountain was a large tunnel.

"I think we have to separate here," said Lieutenant Stillman. "I want Squad 101 and 102 to go north. Squad 103 and 104 will go south. Unfortunately, the tunnel is blocked. It was bombed with a large explosive. So you will have to clime around the mountain. I will go north. I understand that most of the problem is up there. Please keep in touch with your army phone. I am constantly in contact with my superiors. Let's Move on." Sargent Halisek yelled over to Sargent Benson.

"We will take the western side if you will take the eastern side

"I agree, it sounds good to me" yelled back Sargent Benson. They slowly moved up the hill to the clearing. They could see a couple of miles up the clearing. There was no one in sight. They could however see a building not too far from where they were. They slowly approached the building.

"I believe this is the rear guard post," said Lieutenant Stillman. "I think I will set up my office here. You all proceed moving north. Sargent Halisek, I place you in charge. Keep in touch by phone and keep me inform of what you see,"

"Yes sir," said Sargent Halisek. "Let's all move forward." When they had gone out of sight of the building Sargent Halisek went over to Sargent Benson.

"We will work together as a team," said Sargent Halisek. "I Think the captain has to hold some responsible. "Don't let this bother you."

"I understand," said Sargent Benson. "This doesn't bother me. You have been here longer than I. You have much more experience than I have. Actually I feel relieved." Slowly they move forward. About an hour later they came to a spot that astonished Gino. On their left was a big hole that was obviously man made. Inside the hole he saw the largest cannon that Gino had ever seen. They walked down a small set of steps and looked around. On the left side they saw a little cave. In side they found many items that made terrible suggestions.

"I think that they had slave women down here," suggested Andy.

I think that they miss treated the women that they captured somewhere." Sargent Halisek heard the comment and added his own. "I think they got them from the hospital that I was told was located here. I think the Philippine doctors brought patients that they felt had very catching diseases. Looking at the bed it also looks like the victims were sexual abused." Gino went up to the cannon.

"Boy I never saw cannon this big. I think that the barrel is about three feet round " said Gino almost to himself. He then turned to Andy.

"Andy, will you do me a favor. Here is my camera. I'm going to climb up on the barrel and sit on it like I was riding a house. Take a picture of me on the barrel. I would like to be able to show this to people at home. I don't think they would believe me." Gino climbed up and sat on the barrel. Andy took three pictures.

"Let's move on," said Sargent Halisek. "I would like to get up to the hospital before it gets dark." A short time later they reached the hospital. It was located at the east side of the land overlooking the water. It was almost completely destroyed. It was completely trashed inside. As they walked around they noticed a few ropes that were hanging from the beams. At the end of each rope was a loop.

"I wonder what these were used for?" asked Andy. Sargent Halisek, who seemed to be hanging close to Gino and Andy, saw what they were looking at.

"I think they used those ropes to hang the captives," he suggested. "They probable had no other way to handle captives."

"Are the Japanese that cruel," asked Andy. No one answered.

"By the way, before you leave the area, look down at the end of the land to the bay below." said Sargent Halisek. "Tell me what you see." Andy and Gino looked down together.

"It looks like a Battle Ship," said Andy.

"It is," said Sargent Halisek. "It is completely made of concrete. It has cannons on both ends. It was to protect the island. The cannons, on the other end, were to protect the west side of the island." They walked north for about two miles when the phone Sargent Halisek had, rang. Sargent Halisek answered it. Then he turned to Sargent Benson.

"That was Lieutenant Stillman. He has asked us to hold up here. We are to set up the tents and stay until he calls back."

"Is there a problem up ahead?" asked Andy.

"I think there might be," said Sar ent Halisek. "I believe that they are asking for some assistance by air of Special Forces to help us." They set up the tents and remained there for the rest of the day. The next day they heard a helicopter fly overhead.

"There goes our helper," said Andy. They were then asked to leave the tents and move forward slowly and with complete caution. As they moved they finally came to the northern wooded area.

"Stay behind the trees," ordered Sargent Halisek. They slowly moved forward. Finally they could see the problem. Ahead of them were hills about fifteen feet high. It looks like they covered across the complete island. There were a dozen Caves under each hill.

"I see why they asked us to hold up on our movement," said Gino. "Look over there on your left."

"Yes I see them," said Andy. "They called for flame throwers. I also hear an announcement from a loud speaker. I don't understand it. I think it is in Japanese.

"Hay Bobby," yelled out Gino to a member of Squad 102. "I remember right, you said that you understood Japanese. If so, tell us what is being said."

"They are telling the Japs in the caves that they can come out on their own or be burned out." Just as he finished speaking they noticed that a flame thrower had pointed to a cave and fired. Immediately, two Japanese soldiers came out with their clothes on fire. Squad 104 members helped them put out the fire to save them.

"Let's move up," ordered Sargent Halisek. They moved forward keeping a tree or at least a shrub between them and the cave they were approaching. They noticed that on the far right some of the Japanese were leaving their cave and surrendering. They came out with their hands in the air. Suddenly Gino noticed that two Japanese soldiers came out of the cave Squad 101 was watching. They came out with their hands in the air. One of the soldiers walked closely behind his companion almost hiding behind him. Gino and Andy got up and approached them to take them prisoners. Suddenly Sargent Halisek came running toward them yelling.

"Take cover," he yelled at his men while firing his gun at the two men that were surrendering. Gino's first thoughts were that the Sargent had gone mad. Why would he kill the po r solders that were surrendering? As soon as the men fe l to the ground dead from the multitude of bullets they received, Gino realized what the Sargent was doing. The man in front had a machine gun strapped to his back. The idea was that as soon as they got close enough the man in front would bend over and the man behind him would fire the machine gun eliminating their enemies. Gino and the others were in a state of shock.

"How in the world did you know about their plans?" asked George one of the quad members.

"I have been in this war for every," said Sargent Halisek. "Besides didn't you see the heavy straps around the man in front?"

A few minutes after the men were removed a young Japanese soldier came walking out of the same cave.

Please don't shot," He said. "I surrender."

"You speak perfect English said Andy. "Where are you from?"

"I am American born," he answered. "I was born in San Francisco.

"What are you doing in the Japanese army?"

"When I was twelve years old my parents moved back to Japan where they came from before I was born. My name is Benji. I had no choice. I was drafted. I would like to regain my citizenship status."

"We can't do anything about that," said Andy. "You will have to negotiate that with our superiors." Andy tied his hands and delivered him to the group that was handling prisoners.

They eventually cleared the area. They had taken six prisoners. A few minutes later two helicopters came. The prisoners with their hands bounded tight were taken to the Army stockade in Luzon. Gino was thinking about the past hours. He realized that Sargent Halisek had saved his life. He also felt pleased that as yet he had not killed or even fired a shot at any one. After a final search they were marched back to the boats. After they reach land again they were marched back to the basic camp where all their possessions were. Andy and Gino sat down and discussed the past events.

"I wonder what our next assignment will be," said Gino.

"I think that we will eventually be shipped to the action in northern Luzon," responded Andy.

"You are probably right," agreed Gino. After a few minutes, both being very tired from their trip from Corregidor, decided to go to bed. Gino lay in bed trying to imagine what the rest of his live in the service would be like. Never in a life time would Gino have guessed what the future had in store for him In the Philippines.

CHAPTER FOUR

Unsuspected Turn of Events

The next few days went by slowly. The men were assembled every morning to do the standard exercises that they had been doing. This they were told was to keep them in fighting shape. Each squad was also assigned a week as waterfront guards. They didn't want Japanese sneaking in from the west coast just be ow manila bay. Andy and Gino spent time together. They were like brothers. A couple of evenings they went to the movies. A couple of afternoons they spent time with boys from squad 104 who always had a card game going on. It was on the holiday week that Gino's squad was assigned guard duty. Gino spent Christmas Eve pacing up and down the waterfront looking out towards manila bay. He spent New Year's Eve also on guard duty. His schedule that day was from four to midnight. When he got to the barracks, after his tour of duty he found that several of the men were celebrating New Year getting high on alcohol. Gino could see the bottles but the name on the bottles were not written in English. Gino joined them.

"Happy New Year Gino," said Ben. "Come and joined the party. Ben then offered Gino a glass of the liquor they were drinking

"No thank you," said Gino. "I don't drink stuff like that."

"Afraid that you can't handle it?" said Ralph.

"I'm Italian," said Gino. "I'm a wine drinker."

"That is an excuse," said Ralph. "I dare you to take two of these shot glasses. They are only one ounce glasses. Gino seeing all the laughter and jolly atmosphere he started to get into the party mood. However he did not realize that the glasses were two ounce glasses. He accepted the drinks. It was only a short time later that Gino began to feel the effects of the drinks. However he was determined not to show them that he was getting high. Every movement he made he did with strong concentration. One time he excused himself to go the rest room. He went behind the building to let time go by and let the feeling subside a little. Every step he took was with concentration on ever muscle in his legs and body he had to move. The evening went by to slowly for Gino. Finally every one became too tired to continue and they all went back to their own beds. It was about four in the morning. The next day when Gino went in for breakfast he met Ben.

"I can believe that four ounces of alcohol didn't affect you," said Ben. "I thought you were going to pass out and I would have had to carry you to your bed." The rest of the week he heard the same thing from the others in the post.

It was on Monday of the second month since they got back from Corregidor that all the squads were ass mbled in the morning as usual. Normally the squads are about a hundred feet apart. This morning they were all marched together in front of squad 103's barrack. They were all talking, wondering what was going on. Lieutenant Stillman called them all to attention.

"Listen up fellows," he started. "We have been given instructions from Colonel Becker. We are all going on new assignments. Will the following personnel please step forward? Sargent Halisek, Private Eugene Graven from Squad 102, Private Michael Burdon from squad 103, Private Benjamin Selmer from squad 104, Ralph Gordon from squad 104 and Private Gino Cozano from squad 101. Will these six please gather your possessions and proceed to the field west of the barracks and wait for further instructions. Sargent Barner of squad 103, I am asking you to take over squad 101 in place of Sargent Halisek. Will Private Joseph Granger join squad 101? This completes squad 101. Will squad 101 gather your belongings and line up in front of Barracks 1. Will Private John Kolowski join squad two? This completes squad 102. Will you gather your belongings and line up in front of barrack 2. Will private Norman Franken and David Linger join squad 104? This completes squad 104. Please gather up your belongings and line up in front of barracks 3. Will Private James Gena please step forward?, I want you and the remaining members of squad 103 to gather your belongings and proceed to the field west of the barrack and wait for further instructions." After they left he asked Squads 101,102, and 104 to gather around him. "We are Platoon 4. We will only have three squads in this Platoon. We are to be shipped to the northern area of Luzon. We are to join the forces that are fighting there." He then asked them to proceed to the truck and wait for him. "I need to direct the 12 at the west field. I will be just a few minutes. I'll be going with you as the commander of Platoon 4." Lieutenant Stillman then went to the twelve soldiers that were waiting in the west field.

"Fellows I have great news," he said to start his information. "First I would like to inform you that you are no longer members of the 743 AAA gun Battalion. You are all being transferred to the Adjutant Generals Department. Private James Gena, you are to be promoted to Corporal. Your five men under you will be elevated to Private First Class. You and your five men will be assigned as guards at the Paranaque Army Post. You will report to Captain Riso. You will replace the guards that now have enough points to go home."

"What is this about points?" asked Sargent Halisek. "How do we get points?

"It is something that they started since the end of the European war and the surrender of the Japanese. It gives you a point for every month you have spent in the service. The number of point you need changes every month so I can't tell you how much it is. All I can tell you is that it is based on the number of months you have served."

"Will they let you know when you have reached the number," asked one of the solders.

"I'm sure they will," he answered. "Now here is the Assignment for you and your five men. Sargent Halisek, you will be elevated to Staff Sargent. You will receive another stripe above your current strips. The rest of you will become Private First Class. You also will report to Captain Riso. Alright now, here is your truck. It will take you to Paranaque. Goodbye. It has been nice working with you. I don't see that we will meet again. So, I wish you all good luck in your new jobs." After he left in one of the trucks, Sargent Halisek and the men with him all got into the truck waiting for them. They were on their way to their new jobs. They were all in a state of shock over what was happening.

It was late morning when they arrived at the army post. The truck came to a stop at the entrance gate. A young soldier stood as guard. Sargent Halisek handed the guard a letter that had been given him by Lieutenant Stillman that he had received from Captain Bogan. The soldier smiled a very happy smile as he handed the letter back to the Sargent.

"Walk to the building at the other end on your right," said the soldier. "That is Captain Riso's office." All twelve men walked to the building that the guard directed them and as they reached there Captain Riso came out. All the men stood at attention.

"At ease fellows," said the Captain. "You are not here as combat warriors. You are here as government employees. You are all to bunk at one of the barracks. When the fe lows leave the buildings near where your assignment is you can move into them. Now here are your assignments. Corporal Gena you and your five men are to take over the guard post." He then named the five men that were to be under him. They were the five men that were left over when Squad 103 was dissolved. "If you six will proceed to the building next to the entrance gate and see Corporal Benson. He will inform you of the guard schedule.

"Yes sir," said Corporal Gena. "Thank you" He then, with his five men, left for the building pointed out by the Captain.

"Now Sargent Halisek, you are to replace Sargent Noble as head of the Postal office. Private Cozano, you will be in charge of troop movements. You will keep the mail sorters up to date of all the troop movements. Private Graven, and private Selmer, you two will be the mail sorters. Private Burden, I understand that you were a truck driver before you were drafted. Is that correct?"

"Yes sir," said Private Burden. "I was the truck driver for a children's toy company.

"That is great," said the Captain. "I would like you to be the driver for the postal delivery to the Main Post office in Manila. Private Gordon, you will be the extra clerk to be use where needed. Until your help is needed in one of the positions, you will ride with Michael Burden keeping him company. Since you all are coworker, I would recommend that you go by your first names, except of course for me and the Sergeants. Now go and get your detail information from Sargent Noble."

Corporal Gena and his five men were met at the door of the guard building by Corporal Benson. He sat down with them and explained their duties.

"We are set up for three shifts," explained the Corporal. "We have a morning shift which starts at eight, a second shift which starts at four-thirty and a night shift which starts at one AM. There will be two men in each shift. Are there any questions?"

"Yes said," one of the men. "Who gets what shift?

"The shifts will be rotated," said the Corporal. "Your shift will be changed every week. At least that is the way we have set it up. You can change that if you have better ideas. If there are no more questions then let's go to the next step. I would like you all to follow the current guards through all the shifts. To find out who starts where, I have the sift information in a hat. You can then pick a slip from the hat which has the number of your starting shift." They each picked from the hat. "Now you go and get settled in one of the barracks. I recommend the second from here. It is empty for now. It is closer to where you will be working. It and the next five are normally used for troops that are moving through. When we leave next week you can move into this building which as you can see has much better living conditions."

Sargent Halisek and his five men walked over to the building in the far corner next to the postal building. On the right of the postal building they saw the restaurant which was named Beer Garden. It was a surprise to Gino who found out later that the sign was a joke. They did not serve any beer or strong drinks in the cafeteria.

"Hi, said Sargent Noble, "I am so very happy to meet you. You have no idea how glad I am to meet you.

"I know," said Sargent Halisek, "You and your men get to go home."

"We have been here almost since the Philippine island was recaptured by the marines. Anyhow, let's get you all settled. Has the Captain assigned all of you to your positions here?"

"Yes he has," answered Sargent Halisek. We are ready to go to work."

"Great," said Sargent Noble. "I think that each of you should get together with the person you are replacing." That said he introduced all the men with the person he was replacing. Sargent Halisek and Sargent Noble went into his office to get Sargent Halisek acquainted with his duties.

The week that followed gave Sargent Halisek and his mensufficient time to take over. Private Burdon and Private Gordon with the two men they were replacing went to Manila s veral times. At the end of the week they all said goodbye and Sarg nt Halisek and his men took over the duties of the post. On Monday Sargent decided to go to the Manila Post office with the men to get acquainted with all the duties that they were to do. He also asked Gino to go with them. Gino and Ralph sat in the truck rear s ction. The trucks rear deck had benches on both sides. Four large metal frames were attached across the rear deck. They were round on top. Covering the frames was a large canvas so that no one could tell what the truck was hauling. Michel was driving and Sargent Halisek sat beside him in the front seat. They were driving back from the Main Post Office in Manila carrying some large packages and a bag full of mail. They were on the road for about fifteen minutes when they got to a section of the road that was built along the side of a mountain. They were about half way along the mountain side when an old woman started across the road. Michel stated to slam on the breaks. Sargent Halisek then yelled

"Hit the deck," At the same time he kicked Michel's foot and stepped on the gas petal. The truck hit the woman sending her body over the edge of the sloping land on the side of the road. Being used to just obeying orders Gino and Ralph hit the deck flat on their stomach. As they hit the deck they heard the bullets go through the canvas just above their heads. The truck sped down the road at top speed and was soon around a curve in the road.

"Wow," said Gino and Ralph at the same time.

"What just happened?" asked Gino. "Did we kill that poor old woman?"

"That is a very old trick," said Sargent Halisek. "They send someone in front of the truck and when the truck stops they kill the persons aboard and steal whatever they were carrying."

"Wow," repeated Gino. "This is the second time you saved my live. The first time was in Corregidor. I need to thank you."

"You're welcome," said the Sargent, however you must consider that I saved my life at the same time." This made them all smile. When they got back Sargent Halisek reported the experience to the Captain. The captain immediately got on the phone and contacted his superiors. The next day, feeling more confident, he sent every one of his people except himself. They drove to the Main post Office without any trouble. On the way back Ralph made a suggestion.

"I think that they have cleared everything," he said "So while we are all together how about us visiting the southern end of Manila. I would like to say that I was in Manila."

"OK," said Gino. "I would like that two. Do you all have sufficient gun power to protect us just in case things aren't completely cleared?

"We have our pistols and a couple of rifles in the back

"I like the idea," said Michel. "I think if we pull in behind one of the stores there should b an ally somewhere between two build-ings." He then changed directions and headed to the out skirts of Manila. Just as he said he pulled the truck behind one of the stores. There was an ally which led to the main street in Manila. They got out and walked down to the main street. From there they saw some of the large building that had a section in ruins.

"I can't believe how badly it has been damaged," said Gino. They walk up the street about two blocks when they decided to go back. Just as they got back to the store next to the ally they hear gun fire and heard bullets hitting the building near them.

"Jump behind the brick wall of the store," yelled Gino. The glass window had been destroyed and it was easy for them to jump behind the wall. I was only about three feet high but it gave enough protection. Fortunately Gino and Michel had brought the rifles. They began shooting back at the group of men who were shooting at them. When Gino and his men started to shot back the attackers hid behind the fallen wall of one of the buildings.

"I think that there are too many for us to fight back," said Gino. They are slowly moving down the road getting closer to us. We have to get out of here. I think I saw a door there on the side of the store that leads to the ally. We had better sneak out and back to the truck go fellows. I and Ralph will hold them off until you go down the alley." The fellows did as Gino suggested. The door was blocked with part of the roof that had fallen. Eugene and Ben cleared it up in seconds and proceeded down the alley.

"You go Ralph," said Gino. "I will be right behind you." Ralph did as Gino said and Gino followed behind him. As Gino almost reached the end of the ally, he felt like someone grabbed him by the foot and pulled his leg up into the air. He fell to the ground face down at the end of the alley. Michel started shooting down the alley while Ben pulled Gino around the corner of the building to safety. They all quickly got into the truck and drove away as fast as they could. When they were sure they were at a safe distance they stopped to check on Gino's wound.

"How are you doing Gino?" asked Ralph.

"I think I got hit in the leg somewhere. My whole leg hurts, especially my foot. My leg fee s like it is completely numb.

"It looks like you were shot in the foot," said Eugene. "Let me careful remove your shoe." He slowly removed the shoe. After doing that he removed his stocking. "The bullet tore off the heel of your shoe, and it also tore your stocking. But even though you have a black and blue mark it didn't touch your foot."

"Why does my leg hurt then?" asked Gino.

"Well you got hit hard," said Eugene. "It was like someone hit your foot with a slug hammer.

"Well since he is all right let's get going," said Ben. When they got back they informed Sargent Halisek of all that happened.

The next day Sargent Halisek sent everyone under his command except Gino, himself and the guards that were asleep just back from their midnight guard duty. Sargent Halisek made sure that they were all well-armed. When they came back with the mail they reported that the complete area was flooded with American Soldiers. The next week only Michel and Ralph were needed to go to the Main Post Office. The area was completely clear.

The next couple of week everything settled as was expected. Michel and Ralph drove alone to the Main Post Office, Eugene and Ben sorted the mail and Gino kept track of the troop movements. Everything was back to normal. Gino and Ben became close friends. It was at the end of the month when Ben approached Gino.

"Hi, Gino," he said. "I am tired of the food that is prepared here; I would like to go out to eat. They only have three things they cook. I'm tired of the same meals every day. What do you think?"

"What do you have in mind?" asked Gino.

"By your name I would say that you are Italian, said Ben. "I like Italian food also."

"So what does that have to do anything?" said Gino. "I don't think that I have seen an Italian restaurant around here."

"There isn't any," said Ben. "However I heard from one of the guards that there is a local place that cooks great spaghetti.

"What are you talking about?" asked Gino being puzzled with Ben's remarks.

"I hear that the restaurant, just north of the guard's gate has an Italian cook," said Ben.

"It is about four thirty now so you want to try it tonight?" asked Gino. "I'm game." At about five Ben and Gino got together and left for the restaurant. He was right. It was a short distance from the post. They couldn't even pronounce the name let alone understand what it meant. They entered the building and found that the restaurant was on the second floor. They climbed up the stairs and entered the dining room. They found an empty small table and went in and sat down.

"It looks like a nice place," said Gino. "It is nice and clean."

"I'm surprised that there are not more people here," said Ben. While they were reviewing the menu a young girl walked up to their table.

"How can I," she started to say. She stopped in mid-sentence when Gino looked up at her. Gino was shocked. She was so beautiful. Gino felt something he had never felt before in his life. For a second he thought he was having a heart attack. His stomach was in turmoil. Later he realized that he was having what most people referred to as having butterflies in the stomach. He also felt a lump in his throat. For a while he was unable to speak. Fortunately Ben was not affected.

"I would like your Cavatelli dinner and a cup of coffee, said Ben. "Gino do you want the same thing?" When Gino did not answer Ben pushed him on the shoulder. "Gino, where are you? The young girl recovered from her stunned condition and asked Gino.

"Do you want the same dinner?"

"Yes I would like the same," said Gino reviving from his state of mind that he didn't understand. He also, in his condition, felt like his voice came from someone else. The young waitress walked away to fill their order.

"Where are you at?" asked Ben. "You sound like you are somewhere else. What do you have on your mind?"

"Nothing," said Gino. "I am just surprised at how beautiful the waitress is."

"Wow," said Ben. "You must really be hit by the love bug. Is it love at first sight'?"

"To tell you the truth," said Gino. "I really don't understand what I am feeling. I have never been affected this way with a girl. But how can it be anything, I don't know her."

"That's the way love hits sometime," said Ben.

"How would you know?" said Gino. "The other day you stated that you have never been I love."

"I have heard about it from many of my friends and they all acted like you."

"Very funny," said Gino. "Then you fight off any chance of falling in love because of the affects you have seen by your friends. Don't you know that you are missing the thrill of it all?" Before Ben could answer the waitress came and gave each a dish of Cavatelli and a cup of coffee. After serving them she sat down on the empty chair across from Gino.

"Are you going to join us for dinner," said Ben. "You didn't bring a dish for yourself."

"You guys are new to the Philippines aren't you?" said the waitress. "I don't think you have been to a restaurant here either, have you?"

"We are new," said Ben, "but what has that to do about it? What is it that we are missing?"

"It is customary in most of the restaurants in this country that if a person or two men or two women comes in for dinner alone we usually sit with them and keep them company so that they don't eat alone. Although, it is customary for the waiter or waitress to ask permission to sit with them, I forgot. I'm sorry I was distracted by new guys or, I really don't know why I forgot."

"I can tell you why you forgot," said Ben. "You and Gino both were hit by the love bug." It was obvious by the look on the waitress's face that she was blushing. However when she looked up and saw Gino's face she felt better and smiled.

"I don't know what you are talking about" said the waitress.

"Come on now, admit it," said Ben. "You can't deny that you two were attracted to each other."

"You are both very good looking men," said the waitress. "Anyway can I sit and join you?"

"Of course," said Gino trying to get a word in the conversation and also trying to change the subject. "We would be honored to spent time with you. My name is Gino Cozano and this is Benjamin Selmer. We just call him Ben."

"My name is Lea Abella. I'm so glad to meet you."

"We are glad to meet you too," said Gino. "It is such a delightful custom that you have."

"I would like to know more about you," said Lea. "What did you guys do before you joined the Army."

"First of all," said Ben. "We did not join the Army. We were drafted. It was not our decision." This made Lea laugh.

"I guess that we all had times when we were in a place we didn't want to be," said Lea still smiling. "So what did you guys do before you got drafted?"

"I was drafted right after I graduated from high school," said Gino. I worked in a department store during summer. That pretty much covers my life."

"How about girl friends," asked Lea. "Did you have a love one waiting for you to get home?"

"Unfortunately," said Gino. "I have been too busy working and studying. I want to be an engineer." Lea looking at Ben asked

"How about you Ben, what is your history?"

"Me, no," said Ben. "I don't have time for romance. I have too much schooling to go to before I can consider a girl in my life." They sat there and talked for what seemed like a few minutes but over an hour had passed. Gino finally felt relieved from the tension he had felt being near her. He told a few jokes that he was known for.

"I see you have some customers in the table by the door," said Ben. "That is your table isn't it?"

"Yes it is," said Lea. "I couldn't see it from here." She didn't see it because she was sitting with her back toward the other table but mostly because she was entranced with being near Gino.

"We had better Go," said Ben. "We have been here for quite a while. We have to go. You go take care of the other customers."

"Good night," said Lea. "I hope to see you again soon."

"You can bet on it," said Gino as they left. As they walked to the post Ben turned to Gino.

"I think you had better take it easy," said Ben. "I think you are on the path of a lot of pain."

"What are you talking about?" said Gino.

"Don't you think I noticed your reaction toward Lea," said Ben. "You have a very strong attraction for her. Watch out you may end up with a severe heart break."

"I think it is already too late," said Gino. "I am madly in love with her."

"How can that be?" asked Ben. "You have only known her for a couple of hours. I recommend you end it now."

"I will think about it," said Gino. "I must confess however, that I have never felt this way about any one before. I never even dreamt that I could feel this way about any one especially at such a short time." They soon reached their post and said good night.

For the next two days Gino thought about what Ben had warned him about. He didn't want a broken heart. He had seen it happen to a fellow student in high school. It was very sad. However Gino was not himself. He walked around looking like a zombie. The next day Gino couldn't hold back He had to see Lea again. He thought that if he saw her again that he could get over it. That evening he went into the restaurant for dinner. He sat on the last table in Lea's area. It was not long when Lea saw Gino. Gino was thrilled to see her especially seeing a great smile appear on her face.

"Hi," said Lea. "It is so good to see you. I was worried that I would never see you again."

"I was very busy at the post," said Gino. "I have more time now."

"What can I get for you tonight?" asked Lea.

"What do have that is special tonight?" asked Gino. "I trust your choice."

"I just had a serving of German Meat Loaf," said Lea. "It was very good. Although the cook is Italian he occasionally cooks a fantastic meal that is famous in another country."

"I will like to try it," said Gino. Lea left and returned several minutes later with the meat loaf dinner.

"My I sit with you and keep you company?" asked Lea following the company policy.

"I will be very hurt if you don't sit down and joined me," said Gino. Lea sat down with a smile on her face. She figured that the only reason he came back was to be with her. The though thrilled her.

"I guess you realize that I am very attracted to you," said Gino. "I hope you are just as attracted to me."

"Much more," said Lea with a little giggle in her voice. They sat there just looking into each other's eyes.

"Look Lea," said Gino trying to be honest with her. "I don't think I could come here every night. I can't afford it at my Army income. I'll come as often as my income holds out."

"That will be fine," said Lea. "Come and have dinner here on the days you desire the Italian dinner. On the other days why don't you eat at your post and come here for a cup of coffee."

"Will that be alright with your uncle?" asked Gino.

"My uncle is pretty smart. He is aware of our attraction to each other. He only wonders where this is leading to."

"Let's get to know each other before we discus that," said Gino.

"Why don't you give me a detail history of your life," said Lea. "I do want to know you better."

"This is the best meat loaf I ever tasted," said Gino. "Why don't you let me eat and enjoy it and tell me the history of your life? I will come in tomorrow after I eat at the post then I will tell me about my life while I drink a cup of coffee."

"That sounds great," said Lea. "But there isn't much to tell. My parents were killed in a building that was bombed. I was then raised by my uncle Alfonzo. I graduated from high school last month and was planning to go to college to be a nurse. That is it all of my life."

"Being very interested Gino asked, "How about siblings, cousins, other uncles or relatives?"

"I only have a cousin Marcia and her brother Benito," added Lea.

"I'm so sorry about the loss of most of your family," said Gino. The next day Gino had a very light dinner at the post and quickly went to the restaurant. Lea was there waiting for him.

"So good to see you," said Lea." What can I get for you?"

"Just a cup of coffee," said Gino. I ate at the Post. I wanted to ask," continued Gino. "Do you have any days off?"

"I only have been taking off on Sunday, although, to tell you the truth, my uncle would like me to work on Sundays."

"Why is that important to him?" asked Gino. "Is he against religion?"

"No of course not," answered Lea. "He raised me as a strict Christian. However, that is a question I would like to ask you. Are you a Christian?"

"I am a born again Christian," said Gino. "I belong to a Baptist Church."

"By Born Again, you mean that you have accepted Jesus as your savior and are born again in the Holy Spirit. "We don't use that very much around here but I remember the Bible saying that you had to be born again.

"That's correct," said Gino. "We chose the Baptist Church because its entire doings are based only on the bible."

"You don't know how happy and thrilled that makes me," said," Lea. "We are of the same beliefs."

"What Church do you go too?" asked Gino

"Well you would not be able to even pronounce the name but in translation it is called 'God's word'. You see our church has the same belief as your Church, that is, that everything God wants us to know and do is in the Bible. I would like to invite you to our church but you would not understand a single word."

"That's OK," said Gino. "I spent an hour or more every Sunday reading and studying the bible. As a matter of fact, I get up early every day and I try to take about a half hour and read the Bible."

"Why do you want to know if I had some time off?" asked Lea changing the subject.

"I would like to see you outside the restaurant," said Gino.

"You mean like a date?" asked Lea with a smile on her face.

"Yes," said Gino feeling embarrassed.

"Let's continue as we are for a little time longer," said Lea. "I will think about it. Besides I have to get my uncle to get used to the idea of me going out on a date."

The weeks went by slowly. Gino followed the same plan every week. One day the post got a large group of soldiers to stay at the post as a stopover place. Before they left Sargent Halisek called Gino into his office.

"Gino," he started, "I have something to tell you. You may have figured this out yourself."

"I have no idea of want you are talking about," said Gino. Captain Riso was surprised that Gino didn't figure it out.

"What I'm trying to tell you is that I was in the service about two years before you came to the training camp."

"Yes I suspected that you had a lot of experience," said Gino. "But why are you telling me now?"

"I'm telling you now because I have sufficient points to go home."

"Oh, no," said Gino. "I will miss you. You saved my life twice. I will not feel save without you How soon are you leaving?"

"I will leave next week," said the Sargent Halisek. "The reason I'm telling you this is to inform you that I have recommended you as my replacement."

"Thank you so much," said Gino. "I have really enjoyed the job I have now. I hate to leave it."

I have also recommended that Ben take your job, and Ralph take over Ben's job. Michel doesn't need a companion in his trips to the main post office. There is no danger out there anymore."

"Do they know of these changes?" asked Gino.

"No, I'll tell them after you leave. Captain Riso said that I should send you to see him as soon as I had informed you. So go there now." Under a state of shock Gino went to the Captain's office

"Hello," said the captain. "Come into my office. I guess Sargent Halisek has informed you of the changes that are being made?"

"Yes he has sir," responded Gino.

"What he didn't tell you is that I am sending a form to Washington requesting that you be promoted to Staff Sargent.

"Thank you so much Captain. I will not let you down."

That is all Sargent," said the captain. "You may leave now and get trained on your new job." Gino left in a state of shock.

The next day the troop of stop over solders left. However a Lieutenant Goren stayed behind as assistant to Captain Riso. He was a very arrogant officer. His first action was to order that all the post residents perform body building exercises. He ordered the men to assemble at five thirty right after dinner and they performed calisthenics for three hours. By then, it was to late for Gino to see Lea. That continued for over one week. On the next Monday Gino and Ben went to Captain Riso and Complained. The Captain then released an order that at four thirty the men would be free from Army service. The lieutenant was very unhappy with the order. He complained to the Captain. The Captain explained to him that the men on this post are not Warrior men but Army Clerks. We are part of the Adjutant General's Department and have different rules. After this ruling Gino was allowed to go outside of the post for dinner. Gino then returned to go and spend time with Lea. Lea had heard of the problem and accepted Gino back with joy.

It was one evening when Gino was eating that Lea brought up the idea of dating.

Gino," started Lea. "I have brought up the subject of dating to my uncle often during the last weeks. He was concerned with what I would do when you left. I told him that I was aware of the problem and that I was old enough to handle it. I told him that I wanted to enjoy the little time we have. He agreed to us dating but I had to be in by eleven O'clock. He first said ten but I talked him into accepting eleven." As they were talking, Lieutenant Goren walked into the restaurant.

"Lord, help us," said Gino. "That idiot Lieutenant just walked in." Lea turned around to see what Gino was talking about.

"Oh no," said Lea, "that guy has been coming in here at lunch time for the last three days. He always wants me to keep him company. I can't stand him. He is rude, and arrogant. When I am at another person's table he grabs me by my hand or arm and drags me to his table. This is the first time he has come at dinner time. Look at the way he is walking. I think he is drunk. He must have stopped at the bar before he came up here"

"Well he better not do that tonight," said Gino. "I hate him too. He is the one that had assembled us every night to exercise. That's why I couldn't come last week. We complained to the captain and he changed the rules so that he could not do that any longer. I'm sure he hates me too."

"Oh, oh," said Lea, "he is coming this way" He came to Gino and Lea's table and grab Lea by the arm.

"Come," he said. "I want you to sit at my table." He started to pull her out of her chair.

"Hold everything lieutenant," said Gino. "She is with me tonight. She could come to your table after I finish my dinner and leave."

"I over rank you Sargent," he said. "Therefore, she is coming with me." At that he pulled her out of her chair. Gino got up to stop him. He never got to say a word when the lieutenant punched Gino in the face. Gino in a fury of anger and pain got up and running hard he hit the lieutenant in the stomach with his head. He hit him so hard that he fell back toward the window. He fell into the window and if it hadn't been for the window bars, the lieutenant would have fallen to the ground from the second story window. In a daze he pulled himself up back into the room.

"Gino," yelled Lea, "quick, go back to your post. He is so drunk that he may not remember what happened." Gino listened to her and swiftly left. Lea's uncle had seen everything that happened. He called his bar guard and had the lieutenant removed. The lieutenant was told not to return again or he would be arrested for disorderly Conduct.

Back at the base, Gino went into his quarters and told all that happened to Ben. The next day the lieutenant went into the captain's office to complain. The captain had already gotten a report of the action that had taken place last evening. He was ready for the lieutenant.

"Captain," started the lieutenant. "I want you to punish Sargent Cozano. He is guilty of striking an officer."

"I understand that you struck him first and that you were drunk" responded the Captain.

"It doesn't matter," said the lieutenant. "He struck an officer. I want him punished. If you don't do something I will report this to Washington." The Captain knew that he could make a lot of trouble even if he couldn't win. He then came up with an idea. He had just mailed in the promotion form to Washington. He felt he was still in time to temporarily cancel the promotion.

"All right, said the captain "I will demote him back to Private Cozano. Will that satisfy you?"

"Yes, but I would like to see the results," said the lieutenant not trusting the Captain.

"I have just mailed the promotion form. Hold on and let me recall it." The Captain got on his army phone and called the main post office. He requested that the letter that he was sending to Washington be returned at the next mail pick up. "There it has been done."

"I would like to see the letter when it gets back," requested the lieutenant.

"You are trying my patience," said the Captain. "I could report to Washington that you got drunk and started a ruckus at a restaurant."

"Don't do that," said the lieutenant. "I promise that I will not drink and get drunk again." After he left, the Captain called Gino to his office.

"Gino, listen to me," started the Captain. "I have to please the lieutenant so I am temporarily holding up you promotion to Sargent. I am also going to try to get rid of him. After I do I will resend the promotion to Washington. He could cause a lot of problems if I don't do something. So don't destroy anything that has Sargent written on it. Bring me you jacket. I will save it and return it later. Do you understand what I am doing?"

"Yes sir," said Gino. "It doesn't even bother me. I really believe that God will take care of him. I will pray that you succeed soon on getting rid of him. Gino continued the job he had and tried to keep away from the Lieutenant has much as he could.

It was a week later when Gino decided to sneak out to see Lea. He had missed her so much.

"Hi Gino," said Lea as soon as she saw him. "Come in we have to talk."

"Hi Lea," said Gino. "What do you want to talk about? I don't know if I should be here. The Lieutenant was told to stay away from her. So maybe it was meant for me too."

"That's what I wanted to talk to you about," said Lea. "You probably don't know want happened here after you quickly left. My uncle call our bar guard from down stairs and had him dragged out. Then my uncle called our government office and told them what happened. They called back and told my uncle that they had called the American military office in Manila and they were told that your Army Post had called them too and the paper work was in process to ship him up north where the fighting was going on. So you see you will soon be free from him."

"Thank your uncle for me," said Gino. "I had better go. I don't want the lieutenant to know I'm here. You know that he already had me demoted to Private First Class. I don't want him to demote me to Army prisoner."

"They both laughed and Gino left with the promise that he would be back as soon as the lieutenant was shipped out.

CHAPTER FIVE

Future Unknown

A week had passed since Gino had seen Lea. He decided not to go until the Lieutenant was shipped out. It was on Monday the beginning of the second week that as Gino was leaving the food court, after having breakfast, that he saw Lieutenant Goren leaving his office. He was carrying his duffle bag over his shoulders. Gino snuck toward the entrance. Not to be seen, he went from one empty barracks to another. He watched the lieutenant get into an Army jeep and drive off out of sight. He never said goodbye to any one not even to the guards.

"Good riddance," said Gino aloud. Fortunately no one was around to hear him. Gino then went into work happier than he had been for week. That evening he went to the restaurant to have dinner. Lea was there to meet him.

"Hi Gino," she said, "I guess the lieutenant has been shipped to another camp."

"You guess correctly," said Gino. "I don't know where he was sent to but wherever he went, I feel sorry for the people there."

"So what are your plans," asked Lea. "The last time I saw you, we were talking about us dating. I made a deal with my uncle that if he would give me a day off and Sundays that I would concentrate on the weekends. You know that Fridays and Saturdays are our busiest days and Sunday was next. He agreed and gave me Mondays off. Monday is our least busy day. So are you still interested in dating me?"

"You have to be kidding," said Gino. "I have not been able to sleep wanting to spend time with you out side of the restaurant."

"What are you suggesting?" said Lea.

"Well, I have to work on Mondays so after four-thirty, I would like to pick you up and take you to a dinner in Paranaque. We will have a dinner there and wander around the town. I haven't spent any time there."

"Sounds like a plan," said Lea.

"That is not all of it," continued Gino. "I will come to this restaurant on every Wednesdays. Then on Sunday we will meet after lunch and spend the time together. You can pick the things we could do both on Sunday and Monday if you wish."

"That sounds wonderful," said Lea. "I like it. This Sunday I would like to go to the movie theater. There is a movie there I would like to see."

"It's a date," said Gino with a happy smile on his face. He then ordered his dinner and Lea stayed with him till he was finished eating.

"Well I think you should go now," said Lea. "It is past eight-thirty. I have to help clean up. I will see you on Wednesday. Good bye." Gino left, feeling happier than he had been for a while. On Wednesday he showed up as promised. Fortunately there were only a few people there. Lea was able to sp nd all the time with Gino.

"How are you?" she started. "What can I get for you tonight?"

"I think I would like some of your Cavatelli," said Gino. Lea left and returned a few minutes later with his dinner.

"What els can I get for you?" she asked trying to be funny.

"How about a hello kiss?" said Gino kidding her knowing that she would never comply especially there at her uncle's restaurant.

"I'm sorry," said lea joking back. "You have to wait for that and you have to earn it."

Sucks," said Gino. "I was hoping that I could get away with this. Anyway, let's talk about you. I was wondering about your family. You said you have two cousins. Is that all the relatives you have?"

"Yes," responded Lea. "However, I am going to lose one soon.

"Why what is going to happen?" responded Gino sadly.

"No, it isn't anything like that," said Lea. "it is that Marcia is going to America soon. Didn't I tell you about that?"

"No," said Gino. "You haven't talked much about your family. That is why I asked. Please tell me about it."

"Well there isn't much to tell," said Lea. "Marcia met an American soldier and after a few dates they fell in love. He is a Lieutenant in the US Air force. His name is Robert Belanosa. His father is the president of a large corporation. He has sent Marcia money to get her passport and the required documents to become a citizen of America."

"Why did he have to send her money?" asked Gino.

"Are you kidding?" said Lea. "The cost of getting a passport picture and getting the passport and all the document and paper work you need from our lousy government officials is in the thousands of pesos. With our income we could never afford the cost. If you don't get the right paper work done you may only obtain a short visitation rights to the United States."

"That is the worse information you could give me," said Gino. "What chance does that give us? I don't have that much money. My father is a laborer in a steel factory. My family can barely make it day by day. From what you are telling me, I don't think that I could even afford getting you a passport."

"Don't feel bad Gino," said Lea. "I am well aware of that,"

"How do you know that?" asked Gino

"I figured it out when we first met," said Lea. "You are very careful and sensitive about spending your money. You are not the type who has a lot of money and g es throwing it around."

"You are even smarter than I thought," said Gino. He decided not to tell her that half of his Military pay is sent to his parents.

"And don't forget it," said Lea with laughter in her voice. "Let's enjoy the time we have together. I trust God. If we are to be together God will see to it. One thing I learned from the Bible is that one should have patience."

"Amend," said Gino. The rest of the evening they discussed what they wanted to do with the time they will have together. When closing time came Gino reluctantly got up to leave.

"I will see you Sunday," said Lea.

"What time do I pick you up Sunday," said Gino, "and where do I do that."

"I am in the church choir," said Lea. "It has been a custom with us that after church we girls have lunch together. I would like to keep that custom. So you can pick me up at my house at about one." She then gave Gino the address and how to get there. It was not too far from the restaurant. Gino would have no problem walking there. Gino then said goodbye and left.

Sunday Gino walked past the restaurant hoping that she would be there. He then walked to her house. He knocked on the door. She answered quickly like she had been waiting behind the door. She was well dressed having come from church.

"You look beautiful," said Gino. "I have only seen you in the waitress uniform before. "You look like a movie star."

"You don't look to bad yourself," said Lea. "I have only seen you in your army uniform. I'm glad you are wearing civilian clothes."

"I didn't want to stand out," said Gino. "I want to look like everyone else."

"Well, what do you want to do first?" said Lea. "The first afternoon movie is from two to four and the evening movie is from eight to ten. Do you want to see the afternoon movie and then we can spend the evening till dark wandering around the town look for something interesting to do?"

"No," said Gino. "If it is alright with you, I'd rather do the daylight browsing and then go to the movies after I take you to dinner. We can do all the evening browsing on Monday."

"Whatever you say," said Lea. They wandered around the town hand in hand looking into every store. They entered a clothing store where Lea looked at the dresses. Early in their wandering Gino bought some ice cream for both. They were having a great time just being together. At about seven they stopped at a restaurant that Lea had never been to.

"What do you think about eating here?" asked Gino.

"I don't know," said Lea. "I have never been here. I have been to most of the restaurant around here but not this one. But what the heck, let's splurge." They went into the restaurant and each picked a dinner. They enjoyed the dinner. The food was very good. They sat around in the restaurant drinking coffee and shooting the bull. Gino told her several jokes. Lea couldn't stop laughing. At about eight-thirty they walked to the theater. Gino bought the tickets and they entered. As they walked into the viewing are Lea headed for the stair way to the upper balcony. When they got to the stairway it was blocked with a sigh which said in Tagalog: Balcony Closed. Lea moved the sigh to the side and started up the stairs,

"Is this alright," said Gino. "I can't read Tagalog however I can figure it out to mean Balcony Closed."

"That's alright," said Lea. "I have done this before. What are they going to do, kick us out of the theater? We will just tell them that we are Americans and can't read the sign." They got to the top and Lea led them to the far end of the balcony. After they sat down Lea moved as close as she could to Gino. Gino getting the picture placed his arm around her. The heads were almost touching. They watched the movie for a while. About fifteen minutes into the movie, Gino turned his head toward Lea. Lea's head was already turned toward Gino. Their lips were about an inch apart. Gino could not resist the temptation. He moved forward until their lips touched. The Joy and fantastic feelings that filled Gino was beyond anything that Gino had ever felt before. Suddenly Gino lost control of himself. He had no idea of where he was. He felt like he was alone with Lea in a cloud in heaven. He completely lost awareness of time. Apparently Lea felt the same way. She unaware of what she was doing she wrapped her arms around his neck and pulled Gino tightly against her body. They had no knowledge of the passing of time. It could have been five minutes or fifty minutes later that Gino finally got some of his control back. He became aware that he was kissing Lea. He had lost the reason he was feeling such fantastic and thrilling joy. He parted his lips from Lea's lips. He looked into her eyes. He had never seen such a look of love in anyone's eyes. It was shining in her eyes even in the dark theater.

"Lea," said Gino with a very shaky voice. "I have never felt anything like this anytime during my whole life. I didn't even think that this kind of feeling existed.

"I know," said Lea, "I feel the same way. I never even considered that this could happen. I didn't know it existed.

"You know Lea," said Gino. "This is the first time since we met that I could believe that you love me as much as I love you. The thought thrills me to the edge of my heart." Gino hardly stopped talking when Lea's lips shut his mouth. After a long while they finally came up for air.

"Wow," said Gino. "Look at the clock. It is almost ten. I think the theater is about close. We don't want to be locked in here. Dear Lea, I'm sorry you didn't get to see the movie you wanted to see."

"Sweet Gino," said Lea. "Don't you know? I didn't really come to see the movie. Don't you realize that the reason I wanted to come in the afternoon instead of tonight was because I was hoping that you would prove that you loved me as much as I loved you."

"You are a schemer aren't you," said Gino. "This was your plan along."

"We had better leave," said Lea not wanting to answer. They left the theater and walked to Lea's house. Lea's Uncle was not home yet so they stood at the front door saying good night. The good night kiss last almost a half hour.

"See you Monday," said Gino as he left. That night they both went to sleep with a smile on their faces.

Monday, Gino left his office and went directly to Lea's house. Lea was waiting outside her front door. She knew when he would be off duty.

"What do you want to do today?" asked Lea.

"Why don't you show me around your land here behind your house," said Gino. "There is a lot of land back there. How much of it is yours?"

"Most of it is ours," said Lea. "It used to be a farm. My father used to plow it and plant vegetables. I'm not sure what he planted. I was very young when he quit. That is when he got the job working for a builder. He said the farm was not bringing enough to support us."

"How about your Uncle Alfonzo, did he always run the restaurant?"

"Yes," answered Lea. "It was passed down by my aunt's grandparents. It was our other grandparents that left the farm to my father."

"Well show me around," said Gino.

"Not until you kiss me hello," said Lea.

"If I do that," said Gino, "I will never see your farm land

"Will that be so bad?" asked Lea.

"I guess not," said Gino. He then grabbed her and gave her a loving kiss. After a while he gained control of himself and grabbing her arm he led her to her back yard. "Now can you show me you land?" The land was very flat as far as Gino could see. It was over grown with large weeds.

"It is a very beautiful land," said Lea. "Uncle Alfonzo tried to sell it once, but not only did no one want it, but the estimate was less than a weeks' worth of food."

"Isn't this land all yours?" asked Gino.

"I don't know what the law is but since my uncle took me in as his responsibility he has control of the house and land." They walked around the property. Gino enjoyed the fresh open air feeling. As they approach the house on the way back, they heard a voice yelling something in the local language.

"Hello," yelled Lea back in English. The young girl that was on the land next to Lea's understood and called ba k in broken English.

"Hello Lea," she said as she walked up to them.

"Hello Corina," said Lea. "Corina I want you to meet Gino. Gino I want you to meet my neighbor Corina."

"Nice to meet you," said Gino.

"Nice to meet you to," said Corina. "I have heard so much about you."

"Yes," said Gino. "I have heard about you too. Lea has a lot of respect for you."

"Are you guys going to the Spring Festival," said Corina. "I think that is what it is called in America. At least that is my translation."

"Do all the people of the Philippines, learn to speak such perfect English?" asked Gino.

"It was a requirement in high school," answered Lea. Then turning to Corina she asked. "Are you going Corina?"

"No," said Corina. "I don't have anyone to take me. The biggest part of the proceedings is the music and the dancing."

"I love to dance," said Lea. "There is a restaurant at the end of the town that has Music and dancing every Friday and Saturday. Unfortunately I have to work late those days. However it is open until one in the morning. Perhaps we could go there late after work."

Maybe we could go sometime," said Gino. "But, Corina, are you particular who you go with?"

"What do you have in mind?" asked Corina.

"I have a very good friend that I work with," said Gino. "He is good looking but most of all he is very nice. And I think he would like to go dancing."

"I don't think I would want to go on, what you call, a blind date," said Corina. "I would have to meet him."

"Listen," said Gino. "He has wanted to see Lea's farm. We will not tell him about the festival. Let him find out on his own. Just wait here. I will only be about ten minutes." At that he left and returned to the post. Fortunately Ben was in his barracks.

"Ben," said Gino. "What are you doing. Do you have a little while. I am going to see Lea. She is going to show me her farm. Do you want to come?"

"When are you going?" asked Ben.

"I am going right now," said Gino. "Lea is waiting for me."

"I would love to go," said Ben. "Give me a few minutes and I will be with you." Ben left and came back a few minutes later. He had changed his cloths. When they got there they went directly to farm behind Lea's house.

"Hi Lea," said Ben. "I understand that you are going to show Gino the farm. I hope you don't mind my going with you."

"No," said Lea. "You are welcome. I also want you to meet my good neighbor, Corina.

"Hi Corina," said Ben

"Hi Ben," said Corina.

"We were just discussing the Spring Festival," said Lea. Are you planning on going?"

"I don't know what that is," said Ben.

"It's a yearly outdoor party we have every spring. They have a band and we dance on the cement in the center of the city square. Do you like to dance?"

"I love to dance," said Ben. "On Fridays I love to go to that restaurant at the eastern end of the city. They have a band there that plays wonderful dance music."

"I love to go there," said Corina. "I haven't gone there this year, I have been too busy since the holidays, but I love to dance."

"Why don't we walk around the farm while we get to know each other," said Gino. At that Lea lead them down one of the farm paths.

"Ben, what is your duty in the Army," asked Corina.

"I am in charge the Army troop movement department. I provide the location of the each soldier's present location to the postal people. How about you, what do you do?"

"I am the manager of the woman's clothing store in town."

"That sounds like a great job," said Ben. "Since you love to dance are you going to the Spring Festival?"

"You know," said Lea interrupting their discussion. "I'm very hungry. It is almost six. Let's go out to eat."

"That sounds great," said Gino. Then turning to Corina he asked, "If you haven't eaten why don't you come with us. It will be on me."

"I am hungry," said Corina. "I would like that very much."

"I would like to go to that restaurant that has the band on Friday and Saturdays," said Lea." I would like to know how late we could go to eat and dance there."

"That is a good idea," said Corina. "I have never had a bad meal there." After a short walk around the fruit trees on the farm they went to the restaurant. When they entered the restaurant they heard music. There were people dancing on the dance floor.

"I thought that they only have music on Friday and Saturday," said Gino.

"That is what I understood," said Lea. "But look, there is no band on the stage. They must have a person playing a record." As they entered they noticed that the place was crowded. A young lady came up to them and talked to Lea. Gino could not understand the language they were speaking.

"That is fine," said Lea letting the lady know that they were English speaking people.

"She said that they only have two tables available and they were for two people only," explained Lea. "However they were next to each other. "Ben you and Corina sit at one table and Gino and I will sit at the other table." They did as Lea suggested and soon a waitress came to Ben and Corina's Table. After she took their order she came to Gino and Lea's table. While Gino and Lea were ordering their dinner Gino noticed that Ben and Corina got up and started to dance.

"Let's dance," said Gino. "We will watch and when they bring the food we will sit down.

"I notice that Ben and Corina are getting along well," said Lea. "I'll bet that Corina will have a date for the Spring Festival." They danced until the food came and they all sat down and ate their dinner. After they had finish they all went back to dancing. They danced the rest of the evening. When it was close to the time to go home they came close to each other on the dance floor.

"Are you guys having fun," asked Lea.

"We are having a fantastic time," said Corina. "Also by the way I do have a date for the Spring Festival. Ben has asked me to go with him."

"That is great," said Gino. "We can all go tog ther." That evening they all parted with great joy in their hearts.

On Wednesday Gino went to the restaurant. Lea was there to meet him. After getting his order she sat with him.

"It's so good to see you," said Gino. "We had such a wonderful time yesterday. We should do it again."

"I agree," said Lea. "At least we got Corina a date for the Spring Festival."

"And maybe a date for many days to come," added Gino.

"Yes they did seem to get along just great," said Lea.

"What time do we get together for the Festival?" asked Gino.

"I would like to spend all day there," said Lea. "This only comes once a year. Who knows whether you will be here next year?"

"Are you going to church first?" asked Gino.

"I think I will go to church but I will not have lunch with the girls like I usually do. I think I will meet you at eleven in front of the church. We can go to the festival from there."

Wednesday Gino showed up at the restaurant. He decided to have dinner there so that he could spend more time with Lea.

"Hi," said Lea," did you come for dinner? I thought that Wednesday was you cup of coffee day."

"I just wanted to spend more time with you," said Gino. After getting Gino his diner Lea sat with him.

"I can't wait until Sunday," said Lea. "We will have so much fun. I love dancing with you. The only thing that I love better is the time I sent with you at the theater."

"Very funny," said Gino.

"I really love when we dance your ball room dance. You have to teach me more of you dance steps."

"I will try to do that Sunday," said Gino. They sat there the rest of the evening.

Sunday came sooner that Gino expected. He read his bible for the half hour he had promised God and at about eleven fifteen he got Ben and went to Lea's house. Lea and Corina were there waiting for them. They greeted each other and then the four of them walked to the festival. The city square was very crowded. The atmosphere was filled with laughter and joyous sounds. The band was at the far end of the square. The band was playing beautiful dance music.

"Do you want to dance first or go get some food first?" asked Gino.

"That music and the happy sounds makes it difficult not to dance first," said Lea "What do you guys think?" she said turning toward Ben and Corina.

"I see what you mean," said Ben. "But I didn't eat breakfast and am very hungry. Let's eat first and get that over with. Then we can dance until we fall down."

"We may want to play some of the games they have," said Corina." They went to the food court that was outside behind the band. After eating they did all the things that were available to them. Most of the time, however, they danced. The evening went by too fast. It was about eleven-thirty when they left the festival Most of the people left when the band stopped playing. Gino and his group headed home. They knew when they left that they were going to have a good night's sleep.

Monday came too soon. Gino was still tired from the night before. However he was not going to put off seeing Lea. After work he headed for Lea's home. He was about to knock on the when Lea came out.

"Hi Lea," said Gino

"Hi Gino," responded Lea.

"What do you want to tonight?" asked Gino

"I think we should go out to eat first," said Lea, "and not to a restaurant that has dance music. I'm still tired from yesterday. Let's go to a small restaurant and afterwards let's come back here and just hang around."

"I like the idea," said Gino. They went to a small restaurant and dinner in silence. After they ate dinner they sat there with a cup of coffee and talked

"I will never forget the fun I had yesterday," said Lea. "I can't wait for the next one next year."

"I would like that too," said Gino. "However, only God knows if I will be here."

"Let's not discuss that now," said Lea. "Let's just enjoy being together."

"You understand that the war is over," said Gino. "Is there any reason for American troops being here?"

"I will trust God," said Lea. Then changing the subject she added. "I wonder if Ben and Corina are going to continue seeing each other."

"I hope so," said Gino. "They make such a sweet couple."

"Do you know what Ben is doing to night?" asked Lea.

"I have no idea," said Gino. They continued to have small talk until it was time for Lea to go inside. She wanted to be inside so that her uncle would not get negative felling toward Gino. It was already after eleven.

Wednesday Gino went to the restaurant as usual. Lea sat with him most of the evening. Once in a while a couple would come in and Lea would have to serve them. The evening went by as usual. When things go near time to leave lea sat with Gino one last time.

"It is seldom this busy on Wednesday," said Lea.

"Perhaps it is the results of the joy they obtained from the festival," said Gino.

"That brings up a question," said Lea, "What do you want to do Sunday?"

"I don't know," said Gino. "Are you ready to go dancing again. I wander if they have a band on Sunday or the disk jockey?"

"I don't know," said Lea. "We will find out some day, but for now I would like to go to the theater this Sunday. I didn't see the move the last time remember?"

"Do I remember," said Gino. "That was an afternoon I will not ever forget. Do you want a repeat performance?"

"You will have to wait and see," said Lea with a smirk on her face. That Sunday they went to the theater. They snuck into the balcony as they did the last time. Lea didn't see much of the movie that night either.

"The next few months were very similar. On Mondays they would sometimes go dancing and other times wander around town or in Lea's farm. On Wednesday they were together as usual. On Sunday they would sometimes go dancing and sometimes go to the movie. Lea rarely saw much of the movie. Sometimes they would go with Ben and Corina. Most of the time, Ben and Corina wanted to be alone. For that matter so did Gino and Lea.

The months went by slowly. Gino and Lea were more in love then they ever expected to be. They were so attached to each other that it was like they were one person. It was on Wednesday at the beginning of December that Gino wondered about the coming holidays.

"I was wondering," said Gino. "What are your plans for the holidays? What are we going to do on Christmas?"

"I'm so sorry Gino," she said. "I haven't even thought of the holidays. They have snuck up on me so quickly. I guess I should have told you this earlier."

"What is the problem?" said Gino being concern.

"My Uncle Alfonzo promised my Aunt Nicola that he would take her to visit her family every year for Christmas. Her family lives in the farthest southern island of Mindanao. I and my cousins traveled with them every holiday season. After Aunt Nicola passed away my uncle wants to continue his promise. Aunt Nicola's parents lived there. That is the place Uncle Alfonzo met her. She had a brother and a sister who live there also. Aunt Nicola's parents have passed away but the brother and sister are still there. They have two children each. They look forward to seeing us. We are the only family they have."

"So you and all your family here have been spending the holidays with them," said Gino. "Have you been doing this for a very long?"

"As far back as I could remember," said Lea.

"I'm going to miss you," said Gino. "I don't know what I'm going to do without you."

"You and Ben will go to town and have a great time," said Lea.

"I don't think so," said Gino. "I think Ben and Corina will not want me trailing with them."

The next few weeks, up to the time that Lea left, they had the most wild and romantic time. Gino not only saw Lea on Mondays, Wednesday and Sunday, he also managed to see her on Tuesday and Thursday. They did go dancing a couple of time but most Sundays they spent in the theater balcony. Lea still had not seen a movie. The time went by too fast. It was soon time for Lea to leave.

"Lea," said Gino at their last meeting. "Please take care of yourself and come back to me."

"You will get a taste of what I will feel when you leave," said Lea with tears. "I'm sorry," she added after thinking it over. That was not very nice to say"

"That is alright," said Gino. "We will b th have the same problem." He kissed her tears and lips and sadly left.

On Christmas day they had a little party at the food court. Gino didn't feel like going. He couldn't celebrate without Lea. He stayed in his barracks and studied the bible. The next week went slowly. Soon it was New Year's Eve. Ben went into Gino barracks looking for him.

"Hi Gino," said Ben finding him on his bed ready one of his novel.

"Look Gino," said Ben, "Corina and I are going into town to dance until midnight. Why don't you come with us? There will be plenty of girls you could dance with."

"I don't think so," said Gino.

"I'm sure that Lea is celebrating wherever she is," said Ben.

"I hope she is having a good time with her family. I think I will spend tonight reading this novel. I want to know how it ends."

"Well at least come to dinner tomorrow," said Ben. "Corina and I would love your company."

"No," said Gino. "I don't want to go. You and your date go and have a good time. Give her an extra New Year's kiss from me." The evening went by quickly for Gino. He fell asleep reading his novel.

The next day and the next two week were very boring to Gino. It seemed like each day was like a week. He missed Lea so much. He wondered how he would survive when he is sent home. He shook it out of his mind. He didn't want to think about it. Finally the day that followed the New Year came. It was on Thursday. Lea would be at work on that day. After work Gino walked by the restaurant. He looked inside, but there was no Lea in sight. He walked to her house. He knocked on the door hoping that she had just gone home. No one answered. Gino went back to the food court for dinner. He wasn't very hungry. The next day was Friday. He decided to go to the restaurant hoping to see Lea there. When he got to the gate the guard called out his name.

"Sargent Cozano," he said. "I have a message for you. A young lady came by about three and left a message for you. I thought I would wait until you came by as you usually do to give it to you." He then handed Gino the note that was written on a small piece of paper.

"Thank You," said Gino as he took the note. He opened the note and read it. The note read as follows.

"Hi, Gino, we just got home this afternoon. I am dying to see you. I didn't go to work today. I will be home. Please come as soon as you can. Love you, Lea." Gino didn't even stop to comb his hair. He rushed to her house. Lea was outside waiting for him. She must have been looking out the window and came out when she saw him. She ran to him and jumped into his arms. Gino wanted to kiss her but she was squeezing him so hard that he couldn't pull away far enough to kiss her. Finally he pushed her away enough so that their lips touched. That went on for a few minutes until her tongue found his. That lasted for a few minutes more. Finally she pulled away far enough so that she could speak.

"I have missed you so much," she said. "I think I will die when you leave."

"I'm not leaving yet," said Gino. He couldn't say more because her lips prevented him from speaking. After several minutes they both came up for air.

"What do you want to do the rest of the night," asked Lea.

"First I think we should just hold hands and spend time together," said Gino. "Then I think we should go and get some dinner at the restaurant that has music. I want to send the evening with my arms around you."

"Sounds exactly like what I would like to do," said Lea.

"By the way," said Gino. "You didn't give me the chance to tell you how much I missed you. I have been in a daze since you left. I couldn't sleep work or anything."

"Well let's make up for it," said Lea. And they did just that.

It took several weeks before they went back to their normal routine. Monday at a little after four thirty Gino would pick up Lea and they would go to dinner and sometimes at a restaurant that had music. They loved to dance. Wednesday Gino would eat at the post and go and spend the evening at the restaurant with a cup of coffee. Sunday they go to dinner and dance or go to the movies. As yet they have not seen a complete movie. The weeks turned to month and it was soon July. It was at the first Sunday of July when Lea informed Gino of the coming event.

"Gino," she started. "My Cousin Marcia's boyfriend, Robert Belanosa is being transferred back to the US. He is actually being discharged.

"How is Marcia taking this?" asked Gino. He was thinking that Lea might feel the same way when he would leave.

"She expects to follow him as soon as they get all the papers in order. You see Bob's father is the owner of a company that builds part for several home appliances companies. You see Bob's father sent Marcia enough money for her to get a passport, shipping approval and an American visa, plus the cost of the boat fare. You can't believe

LONG AGO AND FAR AWAY

how much it cost to get all of these things done. I could never afford to move to the US."

"I understand that a visa is only good for a few months," said Gino ignoring what her statement was telling him.

"Bob's father is already doing what is needed to get a permanent citizen. I understand from what Marcia has said that her future father-in-Law would guaranty that he had a job for her and that she would not be a burden on the country."

"That is wonderful," said Gino. "What do you have in mind?"

"Well," said Lea. "Bob is getting a military truck and wants to see more of the Philippines before he leaves."

"That sounds great," said Gino. "Are you planning on going with them?"

"Yes, but Marcia is inviting you and me and Ben and Corina if they want to come"

"I am guessing that your brother will be going too."

"Yes and he may bring a girlfriend," said Lea.

"That will make a team of eight persons," said Gino

"Yes if everyone comes," said Lea. "Also we may not come back until Monday, so you have to get approval from your boss."

"When will we leave?" asked Gino.

"We will leave right after the service at Church," said Lea. We will bring enough food to keep us full until we get back." That day they had dinner at the restaurant that had music and they danced the rest of the evening. After they finished dancing that night, Gino went back to the barracks. There he met Ben.

"Hi Ben," said Gino. "What are your plans for Sunday and Monday?"

"Well Sunday Corina and I are going dancing. Friday evening we plane on just hanging around," said Ben. "Why, what do you have in mind?"

"Lea's cousin Marcia's boyfriend, Lieutenant Belanosa is being transferred back to the US. He is being discharged. So they want a last day with all the family on a scenic drive through Luzon. Marcia, Lea's cousin will be following him to the US in a few days. They plan on getting married as soon as she gets to the US." Gino then explained the whole affair with the two lovers.

"I will have to ask Corina," said Ben. "However it sounds like a great adventure."

"There is one more thing," added Gino. "I don't think we will get back until Monday night. We will have to get permission from the Captain."

"Let's do it right now," said Ben. "I see he is still in his office. He must have some special important work to be working this late." They both went into the Captain's office. The captain was so busy that he didn't have much time to discuss it. However he did approve of them taking Monday off.

"I wonder what has him so busy?" asked Gino.

"I don't know," said Ben. "I'm sure it has something to do with the group of men that have arrived this morning." Little did they know or expect what was coming in the next few days.

On Sunday morning at about ten, the lieutenant came to lea's house to pick her up and her guests. Gino, Ben and Corina all showed up. Gino was surprised that all that were going where there.

"Gino, Ben and Corina," started Lea. "I want you to meet my cousin Marcia, my cousin Benito, and Marcia's boyfriend, Lieutenant Belanosa. Marcia, Benito and bob, I want you to meet my boyfriend Gino his companion and Ben's girlfriend Corina. Wow that was a job.

"We are glad to meet you," said lea's family.

"We are glad to meet you all too," said Gino and his group together.

"Now that is over let me explain something," said the Lieutenant. "I will be discharged in about a few days. I am also as you can see dressed in civilian clothes. So from here on you can call me just Bob."

"And you all can call me Gino," added Gino. "By the way we have two of you by the same name. Ben, my companion, and Ben Lea's cousin have the same name. How can we differentiate between them?"

"Well," said Lea. "Ben is really Benjamin, and my cousin is really named Benito. Let's call Gino's companion Ben and my cousin Bennie"

"Let's end all this small talk and get started on our trip," said Bob. After saying that, he got into the truck driver's seat. Marcia got into the passenger's seat in front by her boyfriend. The rest sat in the rear of the truck. The truck was like the one that was in the Amy post that Gino was in except this one did not have the canvas covering.

They would be traveling in the open air. Soon they were on their way to Manila. As the entered the city Gino was surprised of the structure at the entrance of the city. It was a very large arch across the main road into the city. It was so elegant with a drape like design across the top and the sides of the structure. Above this design was a circular emblem. Gino couldn't make out what the figure in the center of the emblem was. Just below this design were the words 'WELCOME TO THE PILLIPINES.' Gino was surprised that it was in English. The structure was square but the entrance was round on top. Each column of the structure was about fifteen feet wide. On top of each column along its length it had what looked like two smaller columns about four feet wide. As they drove through they saw a large building that had one corner that had been bombed. The columns were broken in three places and were being removed by construction workers.

"This is the Business District," said Bennie. "It got hit the hardest." As they went down the street they saw the damaged buildings. Even when the building were still standing the dark marks on the column was evident of the hundreds of bullet that had hit the buildings. A Couple of building had only the front columns remaining, which also were full of bullet holes. As they progress farther down the street they came to an area that was not hit as hard.

"We are about in the middle of the city," said Bennie. "If you will look on your left you will see the City hall. As you can see it was the first building that was reconstructed besides the legislative Building just beyond it." As they proceeded Gino realized that Bennie who was the most familiar with the city had taken over as the guide.

"What is that beautiful Building on the left," asked Gino. "It looks like a king's palace."

"It is the Malacanan Presidential Palace," said Bennie. "I don't know if any one lives there yet." Not far from there they came to another large building. "This is the US High Commissioner residence." They drove down in the north side of the city when Bennie continued. "The building on your left is called the Roos velt Club," said Bennie. "It was formerly called Jai Alai Club." As they continued down the street they came to a beautiful looking Church.

"What kind of a Church is this," asked Ben.

"I don't know what denomination it is," said Bennie. "It is call, Quiapo Church and Plaza. You can see that there is a lot of business going on around it." When they got near the end of the city they came to a large building. "This is the Rizal Memorial Baseball Stadium" said Bennie. "If you want to watch a ball game here is the only place in town. However I think only high school games are played at this time."

It was one o'clock in the afternoon when they left the city. Bob drove around looking for a place to pull over so that they could eat their lunch. It was a few miles out of town that Bob pulled over on to an abandoned field. They found the box called Lunch that was under the seats in the rear of the truck. Ben and Corina grabbed their food package and decided to eat out in the field. They grabbed a blanket that was on the seats and laid it on the ground in the field. Bob and Marcia also decided to eat out in the field. Gino, Lea and Bennie decided to eat in the back of the truck. After lunch was over they continued down the road going north. It was about two thirty when Bob pulled over to the side.

"Look out in the middle of the field," said Bob. "I think it is a fighter plane." The men got out and circled the plane. The girls stayed in the truck. They were not very interested in a fighter plane.

"It's not a fighter plane," said Bob. "It had two engines on the wing. It had one on each side. You see where they were torn out. It looks like some kind of a small bomber. Ben got in the cockpit. Gino took the opportunity to take a picture of Ben at the cockpit. The three of them got into the plane. It had seat for four persons.

"I don't see any marks that tell me whose plane this was," said Bob. "There is a marking on the side but it is so damaged that I can't read it," said Bennie. Lea finally got out and taking Gino's Camera took picture of them in the plane.

"Now I have a picture you and the plane," said Lea. "Therefore how about we get back on the road and get going. It's about three o'clock already." At that they got back in the truck and headed north again. It was about four when they came up to a military airfield. It had a guard at the entrance. What was significant was that there was a large pole that was about ten feet high. On top of the pole was a Japanese Zero fighter. It looked like it was brand new.

"Is this an American airfield or a Japanese airfield?" asked Ben.

"I don't know," said Bennie. "It could be an American airfield and they are displaying the zero they captured or it was a Japanese airstrip that the American's took over."

"The only thing we can be sure of is that it is an American airfield now," said Bob. After that they turned west and headed towards the Lingayen Golf. The trip was all up hill. They got there about six. The first thing they all did is walk to the edge of the hill looking down at the golf. It was amazing. They were so high that the sail boats that were down in the golf looked like small children's toys. They watch for a while and then decided to eat their dinner. All the couples laid a blanket on the ground and ate dinner. Bennie ate with Gino and Lea. After dinner Bob got some logs he had stored under the back seat and started a fire. They all sat around the fire and exchanged small talk. After about an hour went by Bob got their attention.

"Listen to me," he started. "It took us about eight hours to get here. Although we stopped a few places it will still take a few hours to get back. We only have enough food for light breakfast. So we will have to get back as soon as we can. I think you should go to bed early and we should leave here about eight." They all enjoyed the rest of the evening and each got his own blanket and slept soundly through the night. The three girls slept on the rear of the truck and the boys slept on the ground. The next morning came quickly.

"Up and at it," yelled Bob at about seven. Everyone got up and started to stretch. Two of the girls walk down the hill into the woods. When they came back the boys went to the same place. Everyone knew why they did that. Lea was the last to go. After they felt ready they got into the truck and Bob Drove them to the small river that was about a half hour drive. There they all got to wash their hands and face. They ate breakfast there and soon where on the road home. Bob took a short cut that bypassed most of manila. However he did go into the southern end of Manila to drop Marcia and Bennie off at their home in southern manila. They all said a tearful goodbye knowing that they may never see each other again. Bob then drove

Gino, Ben, Lea and Corina at Lea's home. It was about four o'clock when they got to Lea's house. Ben and Corina decided to go into town. They then left, and Gino and Lea were left alone.

"What do you want to do?" asked Gino.

"I think we should hang around here and just relax," said Lea. "I think that about six we will get something to eat and call it a day. I want so badly to go inside and take a shower. We will do that after we eat because I also am very hungry." They hung around and Gino could tell how sad Lea was, knowing that her cousin would soon be gone to America. The time dragged and soon they went had a dinner and afterwards they parted. It was only eight-thirty. Little did either one know the sorrow that was to follow.

CHAPTER SIX

The Long Way Home

Gino got to the barrack and went directly to bed. He was very tired from the activity of the day. The next morning on his way to breakfast he was told that the Captain wanted to see him and that he should go directly to his office. Gino went directly to his office. He was wondering what it was all about. He had noticed that there were several new solders in the area.

"Hi, captain," said Gino as he entered his office. "I hear that you wanted to see me."

"Yes," said the captain. "I have very good news for you. It seems that your days in the service are over. I got notice that you have enough points to go home."

"How soon?" said Gino being surprised with the sudden information.

"Well, the other fellows are being shipped out as soon as they train their replacements," said the captain. "But I have different plans for you. I sent you're up grad to sergeant about a month ago. I just received notice yesterday that it has been accepted so I want you to go the Manila airport US office to see Lieutenant Sanford. I asked him to see if he can put you on a flight to the USA. I asked Michel to drive your there." When you come back I want you to train your replacement. No sooner did he finish talking that Michel walked in.

"Are you ready to go?" Michal asked. Before Gino knew it he was on the way to the US office just on the east side of the airport. As he entered he met the Lieutenant.

"Are you Sargent Cozano?" he asked.

"Yes sir," was all that Gino could say.

"Captain Riso would like me to place you on the flight to the USA. The flight list is full, but let me see if I can find someone you can replace. I see a Corporal Nester that has just been put on the list." The Lieutenant crossed off the name and wrote Gino's name in its place. The plane leaves at eight Friday morning. I will have someone pick you up Thursday afternoon. You will stay at the Barracks that are behind my office. The complete flight personnel will be there Thursday night. We will board about seven-thirty. That will be all Sargent." With that Gino was brought back to the post. No sooner did they arrive that Gino was introduced to a young Corporal.

"Gino," said the Captain. "I want you to meet Corporal Jenson. He will be your replacement. I would like you to train him."

"Sir," said Gino. "Lieutenant Sanford is having someone pick me up Thursday afternoon."

"That's alright. Do the best you can." Gino introduced himself and they both left for Gino's office. Gino did the best he could and at four-thirty he left and went to the restaurant where Lea was working.

"Hi Lea," said Gino when he first saw her. She led him to a table before she answered him.

"Gino what are you doing here?" she asked. "This is not Wednesday." She stopped asking questions when she saw tears in his eyes. She sat down at the table on the chair across from him. She had figured out what was happening. "When do you leave?" she asked.

"I will be transferred to the US camp that is on the east side of the Manila Airport on Thursday afternoon," said Gino hardly getting the words out of his mouth.

"Lea couldn't talk for a while. Then getting some courage back she commented. "I think we have to have faith in the lord. He will see us through this."

Lea," said Gino. "I promise that I will do everything that I can do to bring you to America. I don't want to live without you."

"Gino," responded Lea. "Let's be reasonable. You don't have any money. Your parents have just enough money to survive. You have four years of college to do. Then you have to work several years to get enough money to send to me for my papers, passport, visa and traveling costs. It will be about ten years before it could possibly happen. And that is if everything went according to plan, and you know that problems come up all the time."

"What are you saying?" responded Gino. "I will never give up."

"I know you won't," said Lea. "What I'm saying is, let's enjoy the time we have left instead of forecasting the future. Let's trust in God. If we are to be together he will see to it."

"So," said Gino. "What do we do next?"

First I am going to take off tomorrow," said Lea "I would like you to take off as early as you can and come to my house. For now I would like for us to leave here," continued Lea. "I will tell my uncle that I am leaving. He is no dummy. He knows how we feel. Then I would like us to hang out alone together. And at about six we will go into town and eat dinner at a place they will have dance music. I just want your arms around with music."

"Sounds like a plan," said Gino.

They then did just that. It was after one in the morning when after an hour of saying good night Gino left.

The next day Gino trained the replacement as well as he could at about two in the afternoon he decided to quit.

"Listen," said Gino to Corporal Jenson his replacement. "I have given you all that you need to know. Tomorrow morning after breakfast I will give you a final verbal exam. I am leaving now for the rest of the day. Go over all the information I have given you." A little after two Gino arrived at Lea's house. That day they repeated what they did the night before except they repeated everything a little longer. At about one in the evening, as Gino was about to leave Lea wrapped her arms around him and didn't want to let go. They whispered in each other's ears how much they loved each other. Finally with tears Gino pulled himself and left.

The next morning after packing his duffel bag he went over everything with his replacement. At twelve he went to lunch. When he came out of the lunch room he was surprised to see that a jeep was parked by the Captains office. He assumed that it was his transportation. He went over to the Captains office.

"Hi Gino," said the captain when he spotted him. I'm glad you came here. Are you packed and ready to go home?"

"I am as ready as I'll ever be," said Gino surprised that that the captain called him by his first name. "And Captain Riso, I want to thank you for all that you have for me. I feel like you are more like a friend that my boss."

"I also am very happy to have known you," said the Captain. "Now you get into the jeep with Corporal Torren and had better go before we end up in tears. Gino already felt a few tears in his eyes. Gino got into the jeep and waved goodbye to the captain. As they drove down the road they came to the restaurant.

"Corporal Torren," said Gino to the driver. "Would you mind if we stop here so that I may say good bye to a friend of mine here in the restaurant?"

"Not at all Sargent Cozano," said the driver. "Go we have plenty of time."

"You just wait here I will only be about a minute." Lunch time was almost over so the place was almost empty. Lea saw Gino first. She ran up to him and hugged him knowing that it could be the last time. To Gino's surprise Lea's Uncle Alfonzo can out also after hearing the yell that Lea made upon seeing Gino. When Gino saw the uncle he let go of Lea and extended his hand to the uncle. To Gino's surprise Uncle Alfonzo hugged Gino.

"I promise," said the uncle in broken English, "to take care of Lea like she was my own daughter."

"Thank you sir," said Gino and hugged Lea again. Finally with a very romantic kiss he let her go. Both being in tears he yelled back, "God Bless You both," and he left. He didn't remember getting into the jeep. From that moment on Gino was in trance. He remembered being in bed that night thinking that he was still at the post. The next thing Gino realized was that he was in flight over the ocean. He came to when he heard the voice of the person who was sitting next to him.

"Hi," said the fellow. "My name is Carl. I thing we are going to spend a lot of time together."

"Hi," said Gino "My name is Gino Cozano. How long do you think this flight will be?"

"I don't know," said Carl. "Are you all right? You looked like you just woke up when I introduced myself."

"I'm fine," said Gino. "I didn't get much sleep last night. I had a big going away party the night before."

"Gino," said Carl, "Where were you stationed in the Philippines?"

I was stationed at an Army post that was a few miles south of Manila. The only action I saw was the liberation of Corregidor. Then I was transferred to the Adjutant General's Department. From there I was in charge of troop movements."

"You were lucky," said Carl. "I saw nothing but action. I was stationed at the northern end of Luzon. We fought Japanese and a gang of revolting northern villagers.

"I wonder," said Gino. "Did you by any chance run into a lieutenant Goren?"

"You didn't run across that son of a, you know what, did you?" He was the most arrogant man I had ever seen," said Carl being very upset. "He acted like he was God."

"Is he still up there?"

"No, the son-of-a-gun was killed during one of the battles. It was rumored that he was shot by one of our own men."

"I wonder if he will Rule in hell." After some small talk they both decided to get some sleep. It was about four hours later that they were awakened by the voice of the pilot.

"We are about to land for refueling, so please fasten your seat belts,"

"Where are we going to land," said Gino who was sitting on the window side of the plane. "I don't see any land." After a while he noticed a small island. "I see it now. It looks like the size of a silver dollar."

"I'm sure the pilot has landed here several times," said Carl. Gino watch with apprehension. The plane circled the island several times, and then it went down low and approached the island. Gino was amazed.

"I think it is going to land on the water," said Gino. "If I could stick my hand out of the window I think I could touch the water." The plane came in so low and suddenly Gino saw land. He was pleased to hear the sound of the wheels hitting the runway. His relieve was short lived. As the plane skidded down the runway Gino could see the other side of the island. They were approaching the end of the runway with high speed. Gino was worried that they would skid off the runway into the ocean. However at the end the plane turned and headed toward the buildings.

"We will be here about an hour and a half," said the pilot. "You may leave the plane if you want to stretch your legs, but don't stay out to long. You may stop at the restaurant for lunch if you want something different; however the lunch here on the ground is on you. Lunch on us will be served on the ship after we are back in the air," Carl and Gino did leave the ship to look around. There wasn't really anything to see. After a few minutes they returned to the ship. Approximately one hour later the plane took off. Gino and Carl kind of dozed off after they were in the air. All Gino could see was water. He had seen enough of that. It was several hours later that the pilot rep ated his speech on landing. A Few minutes later they landed for refueling. They landed as it ..0turned out in Hawaii. Gino and Carl got off the plane. They were told that the plane would leave at eight. They wondered around but not too far from the airport. Gino had Carl take pictures of him in front of one of the buildings. After eating at one of the restaurant they got back on the plane. The plane took off as scheduled. It was a boring flight. It finally landed in Los Angeles. California. A military truck met them as they walked out of the aircraft.

I am Lieutenant Townsmen. I am to escort you to the Army Camp near the train station. Please enter the truck. Gino was getting tired of riding in the rear of a military truck.

"I hope this will be the last time I have to ride in the back of a truck," said Gino to Carl.

"I know," said Carl. "I wonder where we are."

"This is a pretty large airport," said Gino. "We have been riding for ten minutes and we are still in the airport area."

"I wonder," said Carl, "could this be the LA international Airport?

"I guess it is possible," said Gino. "However, I would think that they would land in a military airfield." They drove for about a half hour when the cam to an army camp. They could see the train station as they drove by. They were assigned a bunk and they soon went to sleep. The trip had tired them. You would think they travel by foot.

The next morning the lieutenant came into the barracks and yelled "Rise and shine," he said. "Meet me outside in fifteen minutes." After they all gathered, they were lead to a building that was next to the train station. It was an Army depot. It took all morning with questions, paperwork to be filled out, and the waiting in between before the process was completed. In the end Gino was given his discharge document, his final pay check and a train ticket to Cleveland. As he left the building to return to the barracks he ran into Carl.

"Are you a civilian?" asked Carl.

"I guess I am," said Gino, "but I don't feel any different."

"I know," said Carl. "What are your plans for today?"

"Well I didn't get any breakfast this morning so I going next door to the train station. I think there is a MacDonald there. I'm going for a Hamburger and a cup of coffee." They both had lunch as Gino suggested. They sat around with the cup of coffee and discussed their future plans.

"My train doesn't leave until tomorrow morning at eight," said Gino. "How about you, when does your train leave?" My train leaves at noon tomorrow. I have to go south and then south east on another train. I live in Arizona."

"Then we both have the whole day here in Los Angeles," said Gino. What do you want to do?"

"I would like to explore the city right to the left of the train station," said Carl. "It looks like we are in the middle of the old center of Los Angeles. It looks like very old a beautiful architecture."

"Sounds g od to me," said Gino. They spent most of the walking up and down the main street of the city. The admired how different everything than what they were used at their home town. It was about six when they came upon a restaurant that stopped them. What got their attention was the strange name it had across the front of the building. It was called, "Belly & Eye Restaurant." Below it was written the sentence, "Satisfy both while you eat."

"I wonder what that all means?" said Gino.

"There is only one way to find out," said Carl. They both walked into the restaurant. As they got inside they looked at the table and saw the waitresses. Gino was shocked. The waitresses were all bare from the waist and above.

"There is no way that I'm going to eat in here," said Gino turning around to leave.

"Why not," said Carl. "We can say that we were here."

"We can already say that we were here," said Gino. "I will not say that I stayed and ate here." Gino walked out of the door. Carl followed unhappy about it. He wanted to say he ate there.

"It wasn't that bad," said Carl. "The waitress's breasts were all very small. It was almost like they were men."

"Well you can go in if you want," suggested Gino. "I am going around the corner. I saw an Olive Garden Restaurant there. I never had a bad meal at Olive Garden." Disappointed Carl followed Gino to the Olive Garden.

The next morning came fast. Before he knew it Gino was on the train on the way to Cleveland. The trip was boring. They had food in one of the cars but Gino wasn't very hungry. He ate only salads. It was the first time he fully realized he may never see Lea again. Finally the train pulled into the Cleveland Train Station. It was about five-thirty in the evening. He had not informed his family that he was coming home. He wanted to surprise them, besides he didn't want the big fuss they would have made. He grabbed his duffle bag and went out the station. Outside he found a cab. He gave the driver his address was driven home. At home he paid the cab driver and grabbing his duffle bag headed for the front door. His mother must have casually looked out the window and saw Gino walking up the walkway. She ran out the door and almost knocked Gino over when she threw her arms around him. His sister heard the noise and looked out to see what was going on. When she saw who it was she ran out and threw her arms around them both. The next few days were great joyful days. Gino's mother cooked Gino's favorite meals. Every day was like a birthday celebration. Soon everyone became accustomed to having Gino home. Gino was eager to go to college. He was aware that he didn't have enough money to go out of town so he had to check all the university in the local area. He found that all the universities had already started the fall schedule. The only university that had not started yet was Fen College. He went there and after taking an entrance exam he was accepted. He then registered for the fall Quarter. They were starting later because they were on the quarter systems where the other universities were on the semester system. Next he had to get funds. He had to make a few phone calls to find out where to go to get his GI Bill educational aid. He found the place to go and after showing his college papers and a lot of paper work he got his funding. He then went home.

"Mom," said Gino. "I have registered at Fen Collage. I have also got set up to receive Government funding that will pay for school tuition. So I am all set for collage. They also provide me fifty dollars a month for support. I have taken a cab when dad's car was not available. However that will not work once school starts. I need to buy a small used car to drive back and forth to school. And I will also need one to drive to work when I am not in school. I guess what I am asking is can you spare a little for a down payment on a car?"

"What you are asking is for money to buy a car," said his mother.

"That's right," said Gino. "At least give me advice on how I can get out this problem."

"I can do better than that," said his mother. "I can show you how you can get what you need. First do you remember Fred Cinden who lived three houses down the street from us?"

"Yes we went to school together," said Gino. "He was a little older than me. We were great friends. I remember when he broke his leg that dad lent me his car so that I could drive him to school until he could take the bus again. We were great fiends. I stopped seeing him after he got engaged and then married.

"Do you remember what his father did?" asked His mother.

"Yes he owned a gas station down around 93rd street," answered Gino.

"Well his father retired and gave the station to his son," said Gino's mother. "He operates the repair shop at the station."

"That is nice," responded Gino. "What does that got to do with me?"

"Well one of the things that he does in his shop when his business is slow he goes to the junk year and buys a car that has been totaled and too expensive to fix. If it looks good he buys it from the junk yard, repairs it and sells it as a used car. I think that he may have a nice car that as your friend will sell it to you at a reasonable price."

"That is nice," said Gino, "but how am I going to pay for that. I have about one hundred dollars to my name."

"That is the next problem that I will solve," said his mother. "Do you remember that during your service you send us half of your military income? Well we didn't spend it but deposited it in your account at the bank. It has earned interest and is now about three thousand five hundred dollars. I think that is more than what is need for a down payment. You should be able to buy the car and have enough left over to provide fuel for your complete collage years." Gino jump up from his chair and hugged his mother kissing her on her cheek several times.

"I can't believe it," said Gino after settling down. "I sent the money to you to help because dad was only working three days a week. I can't believe you didn't use any of it."

"That was your money. I knew that you would need it when you came home." Gino kissed his mother several times b fore he left. He immediately walked down to 93rd street. Just as his mother said he found the station. He and Fred hugged like lost brothers. They sat in Fred's office for several minutes bring each out to date on their experiences for the last several years. After several minutes Gino explained to Fred what his problem was. Fred had just repaired a 1940 Oldsmobile. He gave it to Gino for his costs. They parted as life time friends. The next day Gino went to the auto license burrow and obtained a license. Gino was now ready to go to school.

The first thing Gino did that week end was to write a letter to Lea. He explained how much he missed her. After much romantic lines he explained what he had accomplished.

Gino started school the next Monday. He joined the, Co-op program. The programs rule was that students would go to school for three months and then go to work for three months with a company who had agreed to the program. After his first three months Gino was assigned to work at the Philco Radio and Television plant in Sandusky Ohio. He was assigned to the test equipment shop. His job was to design and build production line test equipment to test section of the products as they were being built. During his next two school years he spent his co-op time at Philco. During his last job there he got permission to build a small TV set to take home. He was given permission provided he did it at night after his normal job and he would pay for all parts he used. This was acceptable by Gino and by the end of his term he had finish a twelve inch black and white TV set. It was the first TV that his family ever had. They were very pleased with it. Gino and Lea had been sending letters all during this time. Then one day Gino got a letter from Lea. It was not the typical romantic letter. In this letter Lea wrote what Gino was afraid would happen. She ran through the thoughts they had when he was there. She said that it had been almost two years already. It would be at least ten years before they could possibly get together. Too much could happen during that time. She suggested that they both move on with their lives. She said good bye and closed the letter with, May God watch over you. Gino was broken hearted all over again. He wrote two more letters after that but he didn't get an answer. He finally accepted the fact that that romance was over.

During his senior year Gino met Loretta. He met her at a party that was given by his friend Nick. She was very beautiful. The next day after the party Gino called her for a date. He was surprised that she said yes.

"I will be delight to go on a date with you," said Lorrie. "However, I have one rule. I will only go out on Fridays and Saturday. My school work is more important."

"That is fine with me," said Gino. "What are you studying?"

"I am going to the Cleveland School of Music. My goal is to become a music teacher. That said they set a date for the next Friday.

Gino and Lorrie, as she preferred to be called, became an item. They dated most Fridays and Saturdays. On the day that Gino was to go on a co-op job he requested that he get a local job. They found a local furniture store that needed a Television repair man. Gino accepted the job and therefore remained in the area so he could keep on seeing Lorrie. On bad winter days Lorrie would not let Gino come to her apartment. The days went by too quickly. It was in early February when Gino told Lorrie that he loved her. He didn't feel the butter-flies or lump in his throat as he had felt with Lea but he convinced himself that that felling was a teen age thing and that it didn't hap-pen to adults. She said that she loved him to. In early march Gino, not having enough money to buy Lorrie a diamond ring, he bought a cheap Dime Store ring that looked very much like the real thing. One day after a date when the stood on the steps of her apartment Gino kneeled down and opened the box containing the ring

"Lorrie," Gino started. "I love you very much. Will you marry me?"

"Yes I will marry you," she said. Gino put the ring on her finger and explained that it wasn't real and that after he got a job he would replace it with the real thing. "But do you realize that we have a problem," she added. "Do you understand that we can't get married any time soon? How soon will we have enough money to have a wed-ding, go on a honey noon and find somewhere to live.

"I understand that," said Gino. "But that doesn't change the fact that I love you and want to marry you. I will wait as long as it takes."

The next week Gino took her home to meet his parents. After many visits Gino felt that his family was having a hard time accept-ing her. Gino understood because his mother had told him when he first came home from the army that she prayed that he would marry an Italian girl. Finally graduation came. All his family came to the graduation. His graduation envelope however was empty. He would not get his diploma until he got a few more points. It was because Gino took one more co-op job then need. He signed up for a couple of courses during the summer to get enough points. Lorrie graduated a month later. After the graduation she and Gino went out for a last time. She had to leave the next morning. That night after spending the evening dining and dancing, Gino took her to her apartment. They stopped at her front door to say goodbye.

"I am going to miss you so much," said Gino. The though went through his mind of when he had said goodbye to Lea. The thought made this parting even more painful. Before she could speak Gino kissed her. They stood there several minutes kissing passionately.

"Gino," said Lorrie pulling away. "I promise that I and my parents will work hard on making arrangement for our future wedding in my home town of Dallas Texas." With that Gino gave her one last kiss and left.

The next three months went by quickly. Gino finally got his diploma. Lorrie and Gino wrote for about two months and then the letters stopped. Gino realized that it was over. What hurt the most was his ego. No one loved him enough to stick it out. Gino then went out looking for a job. He finally found one on the west side of Cleveland. It was called "Designers for Industry." He was started as a Junior Engineer. It was a couple of months after he got the job while that he was in his bed room studying his engineering books that he heard a Ruckus down in his parent's area down stairs. He was wondering what was going on he heard his mother's voice.

"Gino," she said "Please come down for a while." Gino went down and saw two nice looking persons, an older man and an older woman.

"What is going on?" said Gino wondering who they were.

"Gino," started his mother ignoring his statement. I want you to meet Mr. Antonio Banio and his wife Nicolina."

"It's nice to meet you," said Gino still wondering who they were.

Antonio is a distant cousin of mine," continued his mother. "I think his grandmother and my grandmother were sisters. They had the same last name. Any way they just moved here from Philadelphia. They just bought a house in Shaker Heights."

"So nice to have relatives here," said Gino. "What made you move here?"

"My company transferred me to Cleveland," said Mr. Banio. "I work for the rail road."

"Is it just the two of you," asked Gino.

"No," responded Gino's mother, "don't you hear the ruckus down stair. They have two children. They are downstairs playing one of Mary's games. Why don't you sit at the table? I am making some coffee and have some Italian desert." The three sat down at the table and Gino's mother went down to get the kids. When the three came up Sal came up first and was introduced to Gino. When Annette came up she walked up to the table. When she saw Gino she stopped dead in her tracks. She could not talk. Gino's mother intruded Gino. Gino recognized the actions of Annette. It was so similar to the actions that Lea had when she first met him.

"Hi, Annette," said Gino. He was not moved like he was when he first met Lea. He was in full control. "I'm so glad to meet you. I can understand what a difficult time it is to move from the house you grow up in." Annette was still in a state of shock. She had never even expected that a man would have that kind of effect on her.

"Hi," was all she could say.

"I think that Mary and I should take you and Sal around town and show you the wonders of Cleveland," said Gino.

"That's a great idea," said Sal who over heard the conversation. "What do you think Mary?"

"I would love that," said Mary.

"How about you Annie?" said Sal.

"What," she said not following the conversation. All she could think of how much she enjoyed just looking at Gino.

"Are you alright?" asked Sal of his sister. He had never seen her so quiet. She was always the life of the party.

"Yes," said Annie recovering some. "I was thinking of something I want to do." Sal repeated the suggestion that Gino had made. "I think that would be fun," she said recovering a little more. Gino didn't feel the same for her. However he had to admit that she was very beautiful. He thought it would be nice to have a date. He realized that he had no one at that time. The fact that he had been dumped by every girl hurt his ego. He needed someone to love him. It looked like Annie was the one. He also admitted that he was attra ted to her. That Friday they went on a double date. To start out they just went to dinner at a restaurant that had music. Gino didn't understand why but he wanted his arms around Annie. On Saturday the four of them went to the Cleveland Zoo. Annie and Sal were very impressed. They had been to the New York Zoo but this one was better arranged. They went out for several weeks mostly on Fridays. A couple of Saturdays they went on picnics. Later they started to go to dinner and after dinner they would go to the Crystal Ball Room. Gino always loved dancing and apparently so did Annie. Gino loved the way Annie hugged him with such passion. Sal and Mary didn't like dancing as much as Gino and Annie. Everyone was aware that Annie was crazy in love with Gino. They didn't want to leave them alone. However on the next Friday Sal and Mary declined going with them. They were sick and tired of dancing. They said that they had plans of their own. Gino and Annie went alone. After dining and dancing it was time to go home. Gino pulled into driveway of Annie's home. Gino wanted to kiss her very much.

"Annie," said Gino. "Let's sit here for a little while. I would like some time alone with you. Also I think we need to talk. I don't think you know this but I am not Catholic. I am a Born Again Christian. I go to a Baptist Church. The Catholic Church varies to far from the Bible. The Baptist church sticks strictly to the Bible. I have a write up, that my father made for us, which show the places where the Catholic Church varies from the Bible. I can show that to you and you can check it with your bible."

"That won't be necessary. I know that you are a loyal Christian. Your actions show that to me. I trust you."

Now with that aside," said Gino. "I would like to just sit here and spend quite time with you."

"I would like that too," said Annie. Slowly Gino reach over to kiss her. She didn't resist. As they kissed Gino could feel the effect it had on Annie. He put his arms around her. Her arms were bear. Soon he could feel the goose pimples on her arms. Her body suddenly started to shake. For a while her arms seemed to fall to her side, like she was just about to pass out. Then she came back to life and she squished Gino so hard that he could hardly breathe. However he found that he enjoyed it very much. He couldn't remember how

Lea's kisses were but this was pretty close. They repeated this several times. After the kiss they never said anything except good night when they parted. Gino did find a change in Annie. She went back to being the upbeat girl she was before meeting Gino. One day after a date they ended up in the drive way as usual. Except this time, after a long round of kissing, Annie wanted to talk.

"Gino," she said, "I think we have to talk about us." Gino could see that she was very nervous. "I would like to know if you care for me as much as I care for you. Am I just another one of you dates. I feel from your kisses that there is more."

"Oh Annie," said Gino. "Did you think that you were just a toy to me? Annie I care very much for you. You are a very special person. I know that I have been putting off my feelings for you. I think that's because I like to take things slowly. Besides I was not worried. You have not been able to hide your feeling for me."

"Gino," she said with great emotion in her voice. I'm crazy about you. I love you more than I ever believed I could feel this way. It started the minute I saw you. It was like I was struck with a disease."

"So I'm a disease to you am I," said Gino laughingly.

"You know what I mean," said Annie while laughing. Gino couldn't help himself. He had to kiss her. After a while they parted.

"That didn't feel like a disease did it," said Gino. "I am very much in love with you. You are perfect for me." He bent over and they kissed until it was time to say good night. The passion between them grew every day. They did spent more time talking during dinner. Gino learned that her brother planned on going back to Philly to college. He wanted to be a Chemist. He also learned that her father was the only relative of Gino's family. He found out that Annie's mother hated being in Ohio. All of her family was in Philly. Her brother and his family and a large number of her cousins were there. The next few weeks went by with great joy. Gino had convinced himself that Annie was the perfect mate for him. She was a Sicilian like him she was a very sweet, upbeat, and very humble. Most of all she was crazy for him. He needed someone to love him more than anything. The days went by. When fall came Annie's brother went back to Philadelphia. He was attending the University of Pennsylvania. He was studying chemistry. As time went by Gino and Annie became closer and more romantic. Gino still wasn't sure that she was the right one for him. He kept thinking of Lea. He never felt for Annie as he did for lea. The magic just wasn't there. When December came Gino wondered about Christmas.

"Where are we going to spend Christmas," asked Gino on one of his dates with Annie. "Are we going to celebrate at my house or your house?"

"I'm sorry," said Annie. "I thought you knew. My parents and I are going to Philadelphia for Christmas. My brother got a job with a drug company and is staying there. My mother convinced my father to go there and celebrate Christmas with her family. So we will be gone for two weeks. We will be back for New Years. My dad can't take off more than the two weeks. I don't want to go. But this will tell us how much we really love each other.

"Don't you know yet?" asked Gino.

"I know for myself but I want you to be sure." Gino was surprised at her answer. She was smarter than he had realized. She must have somehow detected his questioning of their future together. Perhaps it was because he had not proposed yet. Gino realized that he had to make up his mind soon.

Soon it was time for Annie to leave for Gino kissed and hugged her. He saw tears in her eyes. It reminded him of the time Gino left Lea.

It was a week later when Gino came home from work that he realized that he felt miserable. He missed Annie so much. He realized that he cared for her very much. She was a perfect choice for a wife. He went over all her good points. She was beautiful. She was so cheerful and happy. Gino didn't remember a time when she didn't have a smile on her face. And the most important thing was that she was crazy about him. She had no plans for a career. All she wanted was to care for her husband and raise children. How could a man ask for anything else? Gino right then made up his mind. He went into the kitchen where is mother was cooking.

"Mom," he started. "I love Annie and I want to marry her."

"Sweet heart," said his mother. "Nothing would make me happier. Let me talk to her parent to see what they think. Then we could start planning for a wedding.

The next day Gino's mother conta ted Annie's parents. They were just as happy as Gino's mother was. They said that they would be back New Year's day and that they would come over to celebrate the New Year's and perhaps an engagement. When Gino came home from work she told him about the call. Gino immediately went to relative of his father who had a jewelry store. He bought a beautiful engagement ring and a wedding ring. His cousin gave it to him at cost. To Gino it seemed like New Year's would never come. However it came and the Banio family showed up for lunch. Annie came running first ahead of her parents. She ran and threw herself into his arms.

"I missed you so much," said Annie. "I don't ever want this to happen again."

"I will see to it," said Gino. Seeing her parents at the door Annie released Gino and stepped away. As they came in Gino greeted them. "Hi Mrs. Banio and Mr. Banio, it is so good to see you."

"Good to be back," said Annie's father. Then Gino's parents showed up. The women hugged and the men shook hands.

After lunch Gino went into the living room and turned on the record Player. He asked Annie for a dance. She agreed and walked into the living room where Gino was. She expected Gino to grab her to dance. Instead Gino went down on one knee and opened a little box he had in his hands. He wanted to do this before the older folks came in. "Annie," started Gino. "I love you with all of my heart. Will you marry me?" Gino thought that Annie was going to pass out. She grabbed the living room chair to keep from falling. Then as she recovered she threw herself into his arms. "I think that means yes,"

"Yes," she said. Hearing that, Gino put the ring on her finger. The rest of the evening was an engagement party.

Annie's parent's wasted no time in arranging the wedding. They found that June and July was all taken up. The next available date was October. Gino said that he didn't want to wait that long. They finally found a hall on the last week of May. That was great with everyone. About a dozen of Annie's relatives from Philadelphia came for the wedding. The night before the wedding Gino had s cond thoughts. He had thought of backing out of the wedding. Perhaps he should wait for someone who would give him the feeling he had with Lea. Then he decided that it was too late. He could not hurt anyone, especially Annie.

The wedding went smoothly. Gino was in a trance the whole time. He hardly knew what was going on. He did remember how beautiful Annie was as she walked down the aisle. Soon it was all over. Gino and Annie were married. That night when they went to bed Gino felt guilty. He felt that he was betraying Annie. He imagined that Annie was really Lea. That thought came up several times. He tried hard to believe it was Annie. He insisted that the light stay on until they went to sleep. He wanted to look at Annie's face so that he knew who he was with. They didn't have money yet to buy a house so they slept in Gino's bed room upstairs in Aunt Stella's place where he had spent most of his life. It was only about two months after their marriage that Annie got up one morning and told Gino that she didn't feel well. Gino immediately took her to the doctor. After his examination the doctor called them into his office.

"I'm sorry," he said. "You are not going to feel well soon. I'm afraid that your problem is that you are pregnant." He said laughingly. The celebration included the whole family.

CHAPTER SEVEN

Nine months later Annie had a little boy. When Gino went into the hospital bed room to see his wife and son a very thrilling feeling came over him. For the first time he felt a real and strong love for Annie. She had given him a son. From that day on Gino worship Annie.

It was two years later that Gino felt that they had saved enough money for a down payment to buy a house and move out of Aunt Stella's place. After much though and a lot of discussion with Annie he decided to build a house. He got all of Annie's ideas and he designed a house they both agreed on. Then they went out to look for a lot. They found one not to far from Annie's parent's house off of Chagrin Boulevard Road. Gino found the owner and was negotiating a price with him. He wanted more than Gino wanted to pay. It was lucky that they didn't buy it because of what happen on Friday of that week. Gino had been assign to a project that was in trouble. The previous engineer in charge saw that he had fail and resigned before he would be fired. Since Gino was considered the next best, he was assign to see if he could at least bring the company out of the contract without a big loss. Gino not only saved the company from a big loss, he got the job on track and brought the company a large income. Friday morning Gino was called into the president's office. Gino thought that because he had save the job he could possibly be upgraded to senior engineer with an increase in pay.

"Come in," said the president. "Have a seat. I have good news and bad news. The good news is that I am giving you a bonus of a thousand dollars for the great Job you have done. I am also setting your record that you are a senior Electronic Engineer. Now I will give you the bad news. The company is going out of business. We will close in about three months. Please keep this information to yourself. No one will know until we have to lay off all our employees. I'm telling you because I want to help you find a new job. You see when all the engineers are laid off there will not be jobs for all of them around here. There are not too many jobs around here for Electronic Engineers anyway. So I am letting you go ahead of time. You will not officially be laid off until May three months from now. But I will give you the three months' salary and a layoff check. But you do not have to report here after today. Quietly gather you stuff and I will let rumors that you are on a company trip. I'm sorry that it has to end this way. I wish you a good life. Good luck out there." With that Gino left in a daze. Now he has enough money to build his house but he has no idea where. He went home and informed Annie.

Annie," he said I lost my job to ay. The company is going out of business. So I'm not sure where and when I will have new job. She wasn't as concerned as he expected her to be. She had faith in him.

"That's OK," she said. "I'm not worried. You will find a better job." The next day Gino make several Phone calls with no results. Finally he went to an Employment Agency.

"How may I help you," said the young lady at the front desk.

"I'm an electronic Engineer," said Gino. "The company I worked for is going out of business, so I need a new job."

"That is a hard request to fill," said the young lady. "There are not too many companies that do electronic work. And the ones that do are not hiring. I suppose you want to stay in the area?"

"Yes," said Gino. "I would like at lease be with driving distance."

"The only thing that I could recommend that could be hiring is Goodyear Aerospace in Akron. I don't know if they are hiring but it would be worth trying."

"Thank You," said Gino and left. From there he decided to go straight to Goodyear Aerospace. He found the employment office and went in. There was an office on the left and a young lady siting at a desk in front of the office door.

"If you are looking for a job," said the young lady please fill out this employment form. After you fill it out please bring it to me and then sit on one of the benches. Mr. Ballwin will be with you in a little while" Gino sat down and started to fill out the form. He noticed another man and a woman sitting in one of the other benches. Soon a middle aged man came out of the office. He went directly to the other man.

"I'm sorry," he said. "But we don't have an opening for you at this time." Then he went to the lady. "I'm sorry, I check with every department. No one needs a secretary at this time. However, ever so often a secretary leaves, so I will file you form and call you if a secretarial job comes available." He then walked up to Gino. "I see you have not finished filling out your form. Maybe we can save some time. Tell me what type of a job are you looking for?"

"I am an Electronic Engineer," said Gino. He never got to say anything more when the Mr. Ballwin broke in.

"Shut the doors," he yelled out with a very excited voice. We can't let this man get away. We need Electronic Engineers badly." He then turned to his secretary. "Betty, please call Ralph Gunter and tell him I'm bringing him a man to review. Carrying the half-filled form he led Gino out of the office into the engineering building next door. He entered an office and handed the form to the man sitting at the office desk.

"Ralph," he started. "I want you to meet Gino Cozano. He is an Electronic Engineer. I will leave you to review his experience and history. Gino I want you to meet Ralph. He is the Manager of the Engineering Department." With that he left.

"Please have a seat and let's talk," said Ralph. It only took about a half hour of Ralph question Gino when Ralph told him he was hired. Ralph then took Gino around the complete building showing him the labs and all the offices. He also showed Gino his future office. He introduced him to all the other engineers. When they got through they went back to Ralph's office. "How soon can you start?"

Ralph asked Gino. Gino explained that the company he worked for would not close for three months.

"I feel that I would need at least a month to finish what I was working on," said Gino. He felt he needed time to move his family. Ralph said that that was acceptable though he really need him yesterday.

"Where do you live?" asked Ralph.

"I live in Cleveland," said Gino. "If you are familiar with Cleveland I live off of Kinsman Road."

"That is too far," said Ralph. "Are you planning on moving up here?"

"I haven't had time to think about it," said Gino. "I will have to look around here."

"Well," said Ralph. "Maybe I can help. I have a cousin Rosie that runs a Real Estate office. I'm sure she can help you." Ralph then gave Gino the phone number and the address of the office. Gino decided not to waste any time. He went directly to the office. When he walked in the door he walked directly to the front desk.

"Are you Rosie?" asked Gino.

"Yes I am," said Rosie. "Are you Gino? My cousin Raphe just called me about you. What do you have in mind?"

"I was really thinking of build a house. Do you have a lot that I could see?"

"Where will you live in the meantime?" asked Rosie. Renting a place for a short period will b hard to find."

"I will have to drive back and forth until the house is built," answered Gino.

"What size of a lot would you need," asked Rosie.

"You know as luck would have it I have the plans in my car." Gino got the plans he had made and brought them to Rosie. She looked at them closely. Then she took a deep breath.

"You know," said Rosie. "I have another option for you. I have a customer that was building a house not too far from here. The house is about eighty percent complete. He was transferred to Arizona with a big promotion a lot more money. He could not refuse the job. He is willing to sell the house for only his costs."

"Why are you telling me this?" asked Gino.

"I'm telling you this because the plans that you have here are almost the exact copy of the house. Let's go right now and see it. What can you lose?" Rosie drove Gino to the house. It was only around the corner from the real estate office. Gino was delighted. It was a split level design almost exactly like his design. The only difference was that the rooms were larger, and the upstairs bedroom area was extended over the garage. Also his plan only called for a basement under the above ground area. This had a two level basement with a lower basement under the family room which was on ground level. Gino wondered how the builder got away with that. A basement he thought had to have at least one window."

"I like it," said Gino. "How much do they want for it?" Rosie gave him the asking price. Gino was amazed. It was lower than he had expected. Rosie seeing the look on his face assumed that his reaction meant that it was too much. So she added that she could see since they were so eager to sell, if they would take less.

"OK," said Gino. "You see what they are willing to sell it for and I will go home and try to get the down payment in my checking account."

"Also," said Rosie, "I have a friend at the bank that we deal with all the time who I'm sure will provide the loan that you will need." With that Gino went home to explain all that had happened that day to Annie.

The next two weeks were very stressful. They did buy the house. They had to buy furniture before they could move in. Some of the furniture they bought was used furniture. However, Annie didn't want a used bed room. So they bought a low priced bed room set. A month later they moved in. Gino did some work completing the house before he started his new Job. After work every day he worked on the house. By the end of the next month he had all the walls pained or papered. Everything was finally settled and they thought that things would go smoothly from then on but it didn't. Annie one morning told Gino that she felt ill. Gino rushed her to the doctor's office. They found out that Annie was pregnant. He told them that Annie had a problem that was caused by her pregnancy. He said that she had a problem with her pancreas. She will have to watch her sugar level the rest of her life. He prescribed a pill that should take twice a day. Nine months later she had a little girl. Annie's mother's name was Nicolina. Annie thought the name was to Italian for the present age. They named her Nicola on paper. However from the day she was brought home she was called Niche. Everything was normal for a year. In the spring of that year they got an invitation for her brother's wedding. They spent their vacation time that year in Philadelphia. Less than a year later they got a call from Annie's mother informing them that Annie's father was very sick and was in the hospital. They asked the neighbor if they would watch the kids because of the emergency. She said she would be glad to watch them. They got to the hospital just in time to see him before he passed away. He had a heart attack. From that day time went by slowly. When they thought that things would get better, Annie got a call from her mother.

"Annie honey," she started. You know that, except for you, all of my family is in Philadelphia."

"I know mom," said Annie. "Gino agreed that will take you there ever year during our vacation"

"What I am trying to tell you is that I am moving to Philadelphia. What started this is that I was made an offer for my house. I have accepted it and I have to leave this week. I have hired a moving company who will move all of my furniture to your brother's house in Chestnut Hill. It is a suburb of Philade phia. If you remember Sal went to Chestnut Collage." On the day that Annie's mother was leaving, Gino and Annie went to say good bye. She left with tears in both women's eyes. Annie's mother hugged both of the children before they parted. Gino and Annie went home to live their normal live.

The years went by slowly. Gino and Annie became very romantic. They were always hugging and kissing. They were very happy together. Annie got a call from her mother often. One day Annie's mother informed her that her brother's wife had another child. That gave them a boy and a girl just like Gino and Annie. That's when Annie approached Gino.

"Honey," she started, "you know that my brother and I exchange letters often. We have gotten very close through the mail.

He has promised that they will come to visit us soon. I know that you have talked about finishing the area over the garage for a guest room. Right now we have three bed rooms. One we use as a TV room because I don't like a TV in the bed room. The kids both sleep in the same room with twin beds. Joey is going on nine and Niche will be six soon. They will want separate bed rooms."

"Well," said Gino, "the TV room as the pull out couch that can make a it a bed room,"

"Yes," said Annie, "but would you want to have that as your bed room? For a guest's young child maybe it would be OK, but not for Joey of Niche."

"So," said Gino, "What are you asking?"

"I think that you should make two bed rooms in the area over the garage. We could leave the TV room for a guest, Joey could have one of the rooms over the garage and Niche could stay in the room with the twin beds. The other room will be for the guests. When My brother comes, Sal and his wife could have the guest room their little girl Gloria can sleep with Niche and their son Jimmy could sleep in the TV room."

"What would happen," asked Gino, "if they brought your mother with them?"

"We will worry about that when it happens," said Annie. Gino got to work the next evening. He worked every evening after dinner. The area had a wall dividing the area. Gino first built a second wall apart from the other wall so he could make two closets, one on each side. Next he laid the floors in b th rooms. Finally he painted the rear room blue because he knew Joey liked the color. He painted the other room green. It was all done. Now they needed furniture. There was a furniture Store in Canton that had Italian furniture. They were told that two were shipped in from Rome. Annie fell in love with a very flashy set It was not w at Gino liked but he gave in and they purchased it. When the furniture arrived they moved the old Bed room furniture too the blue room. They were going to move joey there as soon as things settled down. A few weeks later Annie saw a sale in the paper and they ended up with a bed room set for the green room. They moved Joey into the blue room. Joey was tickled pink to have his own room. Niche was also happy to have the whole bed room herself. Things soon went back to normal. They were all a very happy family. Sal and his family did visit a couple of times and Gino and his family visited them a couple of times. However as the children got older it became more difficult. As the years went by Gino would sometimes think of Lea. He couldn't forget her. He still loved her. He wondered would life be different if he had married her. He tried hard not to let his thoughts of Lea interfere with his life with Annie. He went out of his way to make her happy. Before Joey's ninth birthday Gino and Annie celebrated their tenth wedding anniversary. They had a house full of guests. They had a very festive day. Gino bought Annie some beautiful jewelry. Annie got Gino the leather jacket he had always wanted but couldn't afford. Eleven months later they celebrated joey's ninth birthday. Joey got a small children's car that had petals to power it.

"You know Annie dear," said Gino. Your son has a very bad problem. He takes apart everything he receives. The car he received he already destroyed. He has slammed it in to the lamp pole and into the garage. We have to do something about this."

"He is just a boy," said Annie. "He wants to test everything. Perhaps he will be an engineer like his dad." Gino gave in. He accepted that he had to be the bad guy if he doesn't want Joey to be badly spoiled. When Joey was twelve he cornered his dad.

"Dad," he said. "I will like to have a bicycle. Don across the street has one and also does Walter. I would like to go biking with them." Gino knowing how Joey destroyed everything he had, to think fast.

Honey," he said. "Bicycles are very expensive. I don't have the money right now. Do you have any money to help to pay for one?

"I have about ten dollars," said Joey.

"That is not enough," said his dad. "But I have an idea, if you are willing to do some work."

"What would I have to do?" asked joey.

"Well back at grandma's attic I have an old bike that I had when I was your age. It needs a lot of work. I think your ten dollars could pay for the parts you will need to rebuild it."

"I'm all for it," said Joey." The next day Gino drove to his parent's house and found the bike in the attic. It was all rusty and the fenders were all bent out of shape. On the way home he stopped to purchase sand paper, paint and the tools to fix the fenders if it was possible. It turned out he had to buy one fender. That week end he instructed joey on what he had to do. First he had him take it all apart then he had him sand the main frame. Joey spent hours sanding the frame. It took a week before it was ready to paint. After painting it he tried to fix the fenders. The one he fixed he painted a different color. They had to buy the rear fender where the license was to be attached. It took two weeks before the bike was ready to ride. Joey, with his father's help, learned to ride the bike in about two days.

"Gino," said Annie about a week later. "I can't believe it. Joey treats that bike like it was his right arm. I never saw him take care of anything like he takes care of that bike."

"It's what I thought," said Gino. "When Joey has to work hard for something he will appreciate it more." Annie understood what Gino was saying and she tried, from there on, not spoil joey too much.

The years slipped by. Gino always showed Annie that he cared for her. Every day after work he would come in the house walk into the kitchen where Annie was cooking dinner and hugged her and gave her a loving kiss. One time they held their kiss longer than usual. Niche happened to walked into the room.

"All right dad," she said. "That's enough already." They all broke down in laughter.

When Joey was seventeen they had a large graduation party for him. They invited all of his friends. Annie's brother and her mother sent gifts and they phoned him to congratulate him and wish him a great future. The beginning of the next week he went to Columbus to enroll in Ohio State University. He was accepted and he was as happy as he could be. He was set on becoming an Optometrist. So he enrolled in the pre-medical program. Being late he got a room at a hotel and planned on going home the next morning.

That night Annie had a bad night. She didn't sleep well. She felt slightly dizzy. That morning about seven she got up to go to the bathroom.

"Gino," said called out. "I don't feel well." Gino got up and went to her. "I'm a little dizzy. I'm trying to go the bathroom but I feel like I going to fall. Please help me." Gino put his arm around her and led her to the bathroom. He helped her pull down her pajamas and sat her on the toilet seat.

"Honey," said Annie. "I feel so funny, like I'm floating in air. My thoughts are on how much I love you. You have given me the most wonderful days of my life."

"It is I that should thank you," said Gino. "Now, no more of this talk. Finish what you are doing and let's get you back in bed." Annie smiled at him and suddenly she started to fall forward. Gino caught her before she fell. Gino picked her up and brought her to bed. He spent the next few minutes trying to wake her. When he failed he checked her pulse. She still had a heartbeat. He picked up the phone and call 911. He asked for an ambulance. He then went into Niche's bed room and woke her up.

"Listen honey," he started. Your mother is very ill. I have called an ambulance. I am going with her. When your brother gets here, the both of you come to the Akron General Hospital." Just then the ambulance arrived. Two men came in with a stretcher.

"Tell us what happened," asked one of the men while the other checked her vital signs.

"She felt dizzy and had to go to the bathroom," said Gino. I helped her to the bathroom. While on the pot she passed out." Quickly the men brother her to the ambulance and place a device on her nose and gave her oxygen. Gino was in a trance. In the hospital he was asked to sit in the waiting room. They took Annie to an examining room down the hall from where Gino was siting. It was almost nine in the morning when they got there. At a little after noon Joey and Niche got there.

"As soon as they got there," niche asked. "What is going on dad?" Gino explained to them what had happen. They both looked worried. A few minutes later a nurse walked by.

"Nurse," said Gino "My wife has been in there for almost three hours. Can you tell me what is going on?"

"All I know," said the nurse. Is that a woman was taken down to the operating room. That is all I know." It was about one-thirty, when the doctor walked into the waiting room. He walked directly up to Gino.

"I'm sorry," he said. "We did everything we knew how to do. She had a stroke. We tried surgery but we couldn't stop the blood flood to the brain. It was probably cause by her sugar level. It was over six hundred. I'm so sorry." From that moment on Gino was out of reality. He didn't know what was happening. The kids all hugged him and they all cried together. Niche was the only one that had some kind of control. She drove them home in Joey's car. Joey was not able to drive. It was the next day when Joey was able to help. They took care of everything from there on. Gino was out of the world. At night he thought that it was all a bad dream. Gino did not remember the funeral. Sal and his daughter came to the funeral. His son couldn't make it. Sal brought his mother. It was a month later before Gino could go back to work. His boss however sent him home for another week

"You are not doing any good here," he said. You have spent all you vacation time so let's call this sick leave." About the middle of the week Gino started to gain control. Realizing what had taken place, he came down with real tears. His kids consoled him through the next two months. When Gino can home from work he would go up to the kitchen expecting Annie to be there to give him a big hug and a kiss. As he walked around the house he expected to see Annie in the next room. It was hard for Gino to except that Annie will never be there anymore. The one thing Gino held on to was that he never stopped going to church. He also saw that Joey and Niche attended with him. He taught them that no matter how bad things g t that they should never turn their back to God. When fall came Joey and Niche asked for a meeting.

"What's up?" asked Gino.

"Dad," said Joey. "We want to know what we should do next. Should we put off going to scho l for a few years?"

"No way," said Gino. "You are going to get the education that your mother would want you to have. You are going to be an eye doctor as you planned."

"We are worried about you," said Joey.

"For the next two years Niche will be here to watch over me. There is no option. You are going to college. You can come home for Thanksgiving, Christmas and New Year. We will be together as a family at those times. The only thing I ask is that you do not neglect going to church." After that discussion Joey realized that he had no choice. When the time came he left for Columbus. He got an apartment and moved in. the year went by faster than they expected. Joey came home for the Thanksgiving weekend. Although Gino's parents and sister came to spend the holiday with them, it went by with little entertainment. Joey also came home for Christmas. Gino sent cards to Sal and Annie's mother. But Gino got no cards from Annie's family. It was obvious to Gino that after Annie's death they had no relatives in Ohio. Gino put up a Christmas tree and bought gifts for Joey and Niche but they spent Christmas crying under the tree. They all missed Annie. Joey couldn't make it for New Year. The second year went by without any problems. In May Joey came home for the summer. It was a festive month because Niche graduated. They were all getting used to not having Annie around the house. Joey got a job as an optician at an optometrist office. Niche got a job at the mall as a woman make up sales girl. Gino now had to go straight home from work to do the cooking. He became an expert at cooking Salmon and Tilapia. For Thanksgiving and Christmas that year they were invited to Gino's parent's house. For the first time they all had a good time. That fall both Joey and Niche went away to college. Joey went back to Columbus and Niche went to Western Reserve University. They both had living quarters near the school. Gino was left alone for the first time. At night after he cooked himself something to eat he tried watching TV. He found that there were not very many programs he wanted to watch. He sat down at his computer and decided to write a novel. Because of his technical knowledge and experience added to a strange thing he came across at his job he decided to write a science fiction novel. That kept him busy until the kids come home at spring time. Finally the next two years went by. Gino and Niche went to Columbus for Joey's graduation. Gino was so proud of Joey. They came home with great joy. Joey spent the summer lo king for a school to study for his doctor's degree in Optometry. He found The School of Optometry in Chicago that he liked. He went for an interview and was accepted. When he got home he went back to work in the optometrist's office. Niche went back to selling make up. That fall Joey went to Chicago and Niche went back to Western Reserve University. For Thanksgiving they both came home. They were invited to grandma's Cozano's house. They went and had a great time. That Friday they enjoyed being together. After lunch Joey cornered Gino by himself.

"Dad," he said. You and mom were the perfect couple. I never saw you fighting or quarreling. Your love for each other was very obvious."

"Thank you," said Gino, "but why are bringing this up?"

"Dad I met this girl at school," said Joey. "Actually she is going to a different University. I met her at a school party, but that is not important. What is important is that she is a good Christian. I remember you saying that I should stay away from a non-Christian person. What I am getting to is, how do you know if she is the right person for me?"

"Well first when you met her did she give you butterflies in your stomach and a lump in your throat? If that is true then you have to get to know her to see if you both could live with each other's faults. We all have faults you know."

"I thought that butterfly in your belly and the other was just in novels not real life. Did you have butterflies in your belly when you met mom?"

"Well your mom was a special and unusual romance. When I was in the army I met this girl that gave me butterflies in my stomach and a lump in my throat. I still think of her. She really was my true love. Your mom felt the butterflies and lump in her stomach when she met me. But I was in love with the girl I met in the army. There are at least three types of love. You loved your mom very much. That is one kind of love. Another type of love is a mental love. That is a love based on very high and extra ordinary respect. Your mother was a Sicilian girl. She was very upbeat. She was very humble and wonderful in every way. You know that love begets love. Her love for me made her a perfect fit. The other type of love is the love from the heart. When that starts out it doesn't matter what the person was like. Now if a marriage turns out as wonderful as mine and your mothers, that's when a part of your heart gets involved, I didn't feel the heart kind of love until you were born. Then I felt the complete type of love. Any way that is my interpretation of love"

"Who was this girl that was your true love and what happened that keeps you apart?"

"She was a girl I met when I was a soldier in the Philippines."

"I guess that I have not met the right girl yet," said Joey.

"I think that would be my guess," said Gino. That afternoon when Niche found Gino alone in the family room she approached him.

"Dad," she began, "I would like to talk with you. Do you have time?"

"I always have time for you sweetheart," said Gino.

"I want you to know that Joey and I are worried about you. When we go back to school you will be alone. You know that we would not be against you finding a new mate. Many of the kids we know in school have Stepmothers. They are all very happy. We would love to have a stepmother.

"That is sweet," said Gino. "But I don't have any one I'm even dating."

"What about that girl that was your true love in the Philippines, have you heard from her? Why don't you contact her?"

"On honey," said Gino. "That was long ago and far away. It was long ago because it was some twenty years ago, and far away because I could not afford to go there and bring her back here. Anyway, she is probably married with four kids."

"Does she have any relatives her in the US," asked Niche.

"Funny that you should ask," said Gino with a smile on his face. "She had a cousin that lived in Manila. What is funny is that she fell in love with a US army lieutenant who had enough money to bring her to America. The funny thing is that his name is Robert Belanosa. You know that it means beautiful noise in Spanish. I can never forget that name."

"That is funny," said Niche. "Maybe you can contact them and see what happened to lea."

"That is long shot," said Gino. "I have no idea where they live."

The holidays went by as they had in the previous years. They spent thanksgiving and Christmas with Gino's family. They spent New Year together, just Gino, Joey and Niche. Gino went back to finishing his novel. It was early in month of April that Gino got a phone call from Niche.

"Hi dad," said Niche. "How are you doing?"

"I'm fine," said Gino worrying since they seldom call from school." What is happening. Are you alright?"

"Everything is fine," she answered. "The reason I'm calling is that something funny happened that I think you will find funny too. I meet a girl in school and I've known her since school started this year. We became good friends. Her name is Melanie. We roomed in the same quarters. I never heard her last name until last night. We both joined a nursing Club. She wants to be a nurse like me. Well, when she sighed in I saw her last name. It was Belanosa. She told me that her mother was from the Philippines. Can you believe that?"

"It can't be the same person I knew," said Gino.

"Who knows," said Niche. "God does funny things some times."

"Well let's find out," said Gino. "Ask you friend if her father's name is Robert and her mother's name is Marcia. If it is have her give you their address." It was the next evening that Niche called back.

"Dad," she started. "I found out Melanie's parents are the ones you named. Their address is in Broadview Heights." She then gave him the address and their phone number. Gino decided that that phone number would not be a good idea. It has been to many years ago. She might not remember who it was. Gino decided that it would be better to just make a quick visit. The next day he went right after work. He thought that he would see them just before dinner so that he had a good excuse to leave. All he wanted to know was how Lea was doing. At about five he knock on the door. Marcia opened the door. Gino recognized her. She had not changed very much. She had a very shocked look on her face. Before he could speak she spoke.

"What are you doing here. Do you want to break her heart a third time." She yelled out in anger.

"I'm sorry," said Gino thinking that she didn't know who he was. "My name is Gino. Remember, we went on a tour of Luzon twenty years ago.

"I remember you," she answered. "So what are you doing here?"

"Why," asked Gino, "are you so angry with me? What did I do?"

"You got married," said Marcia. "You were to wait for Lea. Instead you got married to someone else."

I would guess that Lea is married also," said Gino.

"Your right," she answered. "She married my brother. She got her nursing degree before she got married. They were only married for one year. My brother passed away with a heart attack."

"I'm so sorry to hear that. I have always prayed for her happiness. I have never stopped loving her. I never loved anyone as much as I still love her."

"Does your wife know that and does she even know that you are here?"

If she does she would approve. It would have to be from heaven. She passed away over four years ago."

"I'm sorry," said Marcia.

"Are you going to ask me in," asked Gino. "Or are we going to continue this outside?"

"No, I'm sorry she said as she opened the door wider for him to enter.

"Tell me," asked Gino, "when you first saw me you said that I broke her heart three times I don't understand."

"I would guess that no one in your family told you anything about Lea. Please come in and sit down," she said, "and I will tell you the whole story. After Benito passed away Lea went back to school to learn how to run all those test machines like the Ex-ray, the CAT scan and the like equipment. After she graduated she was hired by the Manila hospital. About two years later Uncle Alfonzo passed away. He left the restaurant and all the other property he had to Lea. Two years before when my brother passed he left all the property we left him and his property to her. About a few months after Uncle's death Lea was offered a good price for her restaurant. She then sold everything she had and with our help here she came to America.

"She is here in America?" said Gino almost yelling.

"Let me finish the story," asked Marcia. "As soon as she got here she got her citizen's papers and her driver's license.

"As soon as we got her a car she drove to the house she had as your mailing address. A young woman answered the door and told her that you had moved to another town and that you were married with two children. Gino, I tell you that she mourned for over two years. Now what did you want to know?"

"What I want to know," said Gino with tears in his eyes "Does she live around here?" and how can I find her?"

"She was working in a hospital here in Cleveland but she recently quit. She is down around Akron interviewing for a new position, as an operator to all that test gear. My husband is out of town so I invited lea to have dinner with me. She should be here shortly. She called to tell me so that I could start making dinner." Gino was lucky he was sitting down. The thought of seeing Lea again was more than his poor heart could take. "You can stay and have dinner with us. I'm sure you don't want to part soon after you get together after all these years." Gino was trying to prepare himself to see Lea. He took several deep breaths. That didn't seem to help too much. Before he knew it they heard the front door open.

"Come with me," said Marcia. "Let's make this a grand surprise." She pulled him into the kitchen. Then she went to meet Lea. Gino kind of peaked around the corner as Lea was taking off her jacket. He was shocked to see that she had not changed a bit since the last time he saw her.

"Hi Marcy," said Lea. "Is dinner ready. I'm hungry. I have some very good news to tell you."

"I have a fantastic surprise for you. Sit down in the couch I think you have to be seated to when you see what I have for you."

"Nothing that you could show me could add to the joy I feel. I was given the position of head nurse of the University hospital Lab."

"I believe this is greater," said Marcia. Hold your breath." She then went into the kitchen and brought out Gino. It was a good thing that Lea was near the living room couch. She held on to it to keep from falling. "Lea honey," said Marcia, "Gino is a widow just like you are. Isn't that perfect?"

"Hi Lea, said Gino. "It is so great to see you."

"Hi," said Lea still in a state of shock.

"I love you more than life," said Gino. With that said Lea ran and threw herself into his arms. She squeezed him so hard he couldn't pull away far enough to kiss her. He wanted to kiss her so badly. After a little while she pulled away.

"Oh Gino I love you too. I never stopped loving you."

"Listen Lea. I will not let you out of my sight again. We are too old to play games. Will you marry me?"

"Is tomorrow too soon?" she asked.

"It looks like I am going to start planning a wedding," said Marcia. "I think that we should have a very quick and small wedding," said Lea. "What do you think Gino?"

"I agree," said Gino. "I would like to just elope but we can't do that for our families. Let's make it small with only our family."

"You should start planning right now Lea said to Marcia. That's what the maid of honor does isn't it."

"By the way," said Gino to Lea, "you haven't said yes."

"Yes yes yes yes, repeated Lea. As she said that, they looked into each other's eyes. With the love they felt, they could not keep from kissing. As their lips pressed together the magic of their love reached a high level. Suddenly everything around them disappeared. They were alone. Suddenly they found themselves in the garden behind Lea's house in Paranaque.

The End

CPSIA information can be obtained
at www.ICGtesting.com
Printed in the USA
BVHW040705240422
634920BV00007B/229